Knowsley Library Service

Please return this book on or before the date shown below

Knowsl@y Council

ROBERTO'S WAR

Roberto's War

Alan Lambert

Pont

For Reuben

Published in 2009 by Pont Books, an imprint of
Gomer Press, Llandysul, Ceredigion SA44 4JL

ISBN 978 1 84851 078 4

A CIP record for this title is available from the British Library.

This book is published with the financial support of the
Welsh Books Council.

Printed and bound in Wales at
Gomer Press, Llandysul, Ceredigion SA44 4JL

Chapter 1

'Look at me! Look!' Aldo's voice echoed round the quarry walls as he climbed to the top of the crane.

'Look . . . Look . . . Look!' He perched on the top and laughed. (He laughed a lot, did Aldo.) Then he beat his chest like Tarzan of the Apes, and dived. Down he went into the still, cold water of the pool. There was hardly a ripple as he slid below the surface.

Freddo and me stood and watched from the little cave that had been carved out of the high sides of the quarry. It was right by the edge of the pool, so we could see him clear as anything, travelling smooth and fast under the water. Like a sleek, powerful submarine.

We whooped and clapped, egging him on. 'Great dive, Al!'

'Well done.'

'Fire torpedo number one!'

With a roar, the human submarine rocketed to the surface. 'WHOOSH!' he yelled, laughing, making us laugh.

And down he went again, down into the rippling water. Three seconds . . . five . . . ten . . . then another explosion as he shot back to the surface. 'WHOOSH!'

'You're a *twpsyn*, you are,' Freddo yelled. In Wales, where we live, that's what you call someone who is acting daft.

Freddo and me came out of the cave to watch him, thrashing and diving and playing, caught up in his fantasy world.

We sat on the flat stone blocks, warm in the summer sun, and dangled our legs in the water. This is where we came to swim. The Pandy pool.

There used to be an old mill round here, once, a 'pandy' in Welsh, so that's how the pool got its name.

When the mill became a ruin, they built a working quarry in its place, a huge hole dug deep into the hillside. You could still see where they'd blasted the grey rocks out of the earth, leaving ledges and steps and terraces that we used as a staircase down to the water.

When the quarry shut down, the owners left a crane at the bottom.

Then, over the years, the quarry filled with water, and all you could see of the crane now was the rusty metal top. It poked clear of the surface by about three or four feet.

So, the pool was our swimming baths and the crane was our diving board. The great thing was, there always seemed to be water in the Pandy pool. Some of it came from the streams that splashed down the hillside, some from underground springs.

The grown-ups told us not to go near. It was dangerous, they said.

You could get caught in the crane. There were hidden ledges that you couldn't see. Openings in the rock where you could get trapped in the dark, deep water.

Children had drowned, they said.

Some kids claimed that the pool was bottomless, but

how could that be when there was a big iron crane standing there? It had to be resting on something, didn't it? They were just out to frighten the little ones, those kids, or just being *twp*.

Aldo turned and powered his way towards us, head just skimming the surface of the water. He was an enemy submarine again, like he'd seen in the films. He sent out sonar signals to let us know he was coming.

'Pying! Pying! Pying!' he went.

Then a splutter and a cough as he choked in some water. More signals. 'Pying! Pying! Pying!'

From our action station on the stone ledge, we tried to blow him out of the water.

'BOOMPH!'

Aldo's submarine changed course, weaving from side to side as the sound of our depth charges echoed round the rocks.

'BOOMPH! BOOMPH! BOOMPH!'

'Got you, Al!' I shouted. 'That one got you!'

'No, it didn't,' he puffed, spitting out water, charging on.

'BOOMPH!!'

'That one did!' yelled Freddo. 'It did, Al.'

'Fair dos,' Aldo shouted back. 'You win. One nil to the Navy.'

He flipped onto his back and paddled slowly towards us, like a damaged sub drifting silently back to shore.

'Watch out,' Freddo whispered. 'He'll try and pull you in.'

Sure enough, as Aldo neared the bank, he suddenly twisted round onto his stomach, put on a burst of speed and reached for our legs dangling in the water. Laughing and yelling, quick as a flash, we jumped up and ran for shelter at the back of the cave.

'Too quick for you, Al!' Freddo shouted. 'Better luck next time!'

'A'right, Fred,' Aldo laughed, still thrashing around in the water. 'But I *will* get you next time, don't you worry!'

Slowly, a bit unsure, we came out of the shadowy cave. Keeping our distance, we sat down again on the big stone blocks to watch Aldo, still laughing, pull himself clear of the water.

Easy. No effort! He was big, strong, much bigger than Freddo or me, and not just because he was older. He was about fifteen or sixteen, I think, and my nanna said he'd grown too big for his own good, even when he was a baby. Sometimes, it had been a real effort to lift him out of his cot.

Aldo was a bit slow, a bit simple, some people said. Which is why he went round with me and his younger brother, Freddo. We were ten, best friends – best butties – but we minded Aldo like he was much younger. He got himself into trouble sometimes because he didn't think things out before he did them.

There was a story going round that one time he squeezed the bottom out of Mrs Pritchard's cat, two doors down. Only, because he was loving it so hard, he didn't realise he was squeezing it too tight. Mrs Pritchard screamed, Aldo panicked, and pushed the cat's bottom back in again. So that was all right.

But you can see how, sometimes, he had to be minded.

'Race you to the crane?' Aldo came padding closer on the warm, grey stones. He flicked himself dry, like a dog, wetting us with the drops from his thick fair hair.

'Oi, lay off, Al!' Freddo shouted, twisting out of range. He didn't look like his brother. He was dark haired and small, like me.

'Too thin by half!' my nanna said.

Aldo sat down beside us, and, for a while, no one spoke. We dangled our feet in the cold, dark water and enjoyed the sunshine.

It was only the beginning of June – but if the weather should stay like this for the next couple of months, we'd have a fantastic summer holiday when school broke up.

After a bit, Freddo said, 'Better go home now, Aldo.'

'Why, Fred? It's not bedtime!'

'We want to go and see the kids from England, don't we? They're coming on the train.'

Because Britain was at war with Germany, children from places in England were coming to stay with us. It was safe where we were, in South Wales, people said. Safer, anyway, than the places these kids were coming from. They were living on the South Coast. Kent, I think. I knew where Kent was because my Uncle Ralph had gone there before the war, to work in the coal mines. They had coal seams there that went right out under the sea, he said. Not like ours that stretched under the ground from one valley to the next.

'Why they coming, Bob?' Aldo started to dry himself on his shirt.

My name is Robert, but, back then, most of my

friends called me Bob. Grown-ups called me Robert, though. All except for Mr Moretti, Aldo's dad. To him I was always Roberto, which I liked a lot. It made me feel special.

'Their mams and dads want them to come and live somewhere safe, Al,' I told him. 'They're a bit near the coast of France where they are – and old Hitler's invaded France, hasn't he? So there's lots of fighting going on there!'

We all struggled out of our wet bathers and dried ourselves off with our clothes as best as we could before we put them on. We hadn't brought towels because our mams might have seen, and then they'd know we were going swimming.

'Who they going to stay with?' Aldo asked.

'People who've got a spare bed, I think.' I put on my daps and started tying up the laces. 'You've got to take someone if you've got a spare bed.'

'Bet Mrs Pritchard won't,' said Freddo. 'And she's got plenty of room.'

'Well, those kids can think themselves lucky then,' I said. 'Wouldn't want to stay with her. Miserable, she is. And mean.'

'I'd like to stay with Mrs Pritchard.' Aldo was struggling to pull on his daps over his big, damp feet.

'Why, Al?' I asked.

Freddo chipped in: 'Because of her cat, innit?' He helped his brother tie up his laces before he did his own.

'Yes,' said Aldo. 'I love her cat.'

Freddo laughed, and stood up. 'We know! You love it

to bits! Come on. The train's supposed to be here at seven o'clock.'

He gave his brother a hand up.

We squeezed the water from our bathers, skipped a couple of stones across the flat surface of the pool – Aldo was best! – and started along the path that climbed from ledge to ledge up the quarry walls.

At the top, the fields stretched away towards our village. Twenty minutes if you walked it. Only ten if you ran. And that's what we did, yelling and shouting, Freddo and me in the lead.

Spy planes we were now, always on the lookout for the enemy from our specially kitted-out cockpits. With our arms as wings, we crashed through the ferns that grew thick on both sides of the Pandy path. Up and down the sloping ground we flew, eyes squinted, always on the alert for enemy agents.

'Are we having kids to stay, Fred?' Aldo puffed as he trailed behind in our wake.

'Don't think so, Al. We haven't got enough room over the shop, have we?'

'Are you having kids to stay, Bob?'

'Yes,' I said, banking hard to check out suspicious activity. 'We are! Worse luck!'

Chapter 2

'Where have you been?' My mother came out of Freddo's café as we were going in. She was wearing her best Sunday dress, with the big green spots.

I whipped my flying helmet off my head just in time. My bathing trunks! I stuffed them, a bit wet, in the pocket of my shorts. 'Nowhere, Mam.'

'Liar!' Mam said. 'You been up the Pandy, haven't you? Mrs Pritchard saw you coming down the path.'

She would!

'We didn't go swimming,' Freddo said.

'Why's he got his bathers then?' She pointed at the drying trunks sticking out of my pocket.

'In case,' said Freddo. 'We might have wanted to.'

'Oh aye,' my mother said, eyes narrowing. 'You're a bunch of little fibbers!'

'I'm not!' said Aldo. 'I'm not little!' He tried to edge his big frame past my mother standing in the shop doorway, but, small as she was, she managed to block his way. My mam could be a little terrier when she made her mind up. You wouldn't want to cross her if she got angry.

'Boys!' she said, not budging. 'I'm only telling you for your own good. It's dangerous!'

'We know, Mam.'

'Well, don't do it then.'

'A'right,' I muttered.

'Fair dos,' said Aldo.

'Right-o!' said Freddo.

My mother stepped aside and let us get to the shop door. 'The train'll be here at seven, Robert,' she said. 'Aren't you going to see the evacuees coming?'

'Yes. We're just going to tell Freddo's mam and dad.'

'Right. I'll see you later. Don't forget we're having a visitor.' And she bustled off down the street to our house.

The bell above the door tinkled as we piled into the shop. The smell hit me like it always did. A lovely smell of sweets and chocolates and ice cream and coffee. Once, that smell had been really strong, but over the last nine months – since the war had started – bit by bit it had got fainter and fainter. Not so many sweets and chocolates around, see, and no ice cream. There were a few glass jars still piled high on the wooden shelves behind the counter, but they were more for show than anything else. Most didn't have any sweets in them.

Coming indoors after the sun, we squinted in the darkness. No customers in today. Suppose everyone was down the station, waiting for the evacuees. That was more fun.

'Hello, boys.' Mr Moretti stood behind the counter, drying cups with a big tea-towel. He was in the black trousers and white jacket that he always wore when he was serving in the shop. 'Where've you been?'

'Nowhere, Dad,' said Freddo, heading through the shop towards the half-open door that led into their kitchen.

13

'Nowhere, eh?' said Mr Moretti. 'Well, I hope the water was cold enough?'

'It was lovely, Papa,' said Aldo.

Freddo stopped in his tracks and winced. He was landed with a brother who always told the truth.

Mr Moretti gave a big laugh that made his jolly face crinkle up.

'*Aldo bello*,' he chuckled.

I could understand the Aldo bit, but I didn't know what *bello* meant. The only Italian word I really knew was *ciao*. That's what Fred and Aldo said sometimes when we were meeting up or saying goodbye. I could tell from the look on Mr Moretti's face, though, that he wasn't telling Aldo off.

He wiped his moustache where he'd got spit on it from laughing out loud. 'My lovely boy,' he said. 'Always honest!'

The kitchen door opened wide and Mrs Moretti stepped into the shop. She wasn't laughing. She looked very stern with her black hair pulled back from her face and her dark-blue shop apron tied tight around her waist. She'd been listening to Mr Moretti teasing us. 'You been up the Pandy pond again, have you, Frederico?' (That was Freddo's proper name.) 'You're silly!' she went on. 'It's dangerous to go swimming there. And you didn't take your gas mask with you.'

Why do mothers go on at you the whole time? Everyone was supposed to carry their gas masks with them at all times in case of a gas attack, but most of us kids never did.

'We're going to go down the station, Mamma.' Freddo swiftly changed the subject.

'To see the English boys,' said Aldo.

'You think they'll look different, son?' his father teased him again, reaching up to stack one of the cups on the shelf behind the sink.

'I dunno. Will they?' Aldo asked, confused.

'Stop teasing him, Dad,' said Freddo. 'They won't look any different to us Welsh boys, Al.'

'I'm not Welsh,' said Aldo. 'I'm Italian.'

The Morettis had come all the way from Italy. It was very, very poor where they lived, Mr Moretti had told me once. His family had all been farmers but there wasn't enough land to go round. So Mr Moretti and his two younger brothers had sold up their little bit of land and had travelled all the way to South Wales to open up ice-cream shops and cafés in the valleys.

There were Italian cafés in all the villages round here. 'Bracchi' shops, people called them. I suppose that the Bracchis had been one of the first families to arrive. I couldn't help thinking that it must have been really poor in their part of Italy if they thought there was money to be made here. We thought there couldn't be many people poorer than us.

'You're Welsh now!' Mrs Moretti moved along the front of the counter. She almost spat the words at Aldo.

Why so sharp? I wondered.

'Remember that!' she went on, busying herself by straightening the little cardboard price lists that stood on the counter top. 'You're Welsh!'

'Shush, Lena,' Mr Moretti said, softly. 'No need to be so hard on the boy. He's Welsh . . . *and* Italian. Still. Half and half.'

Mrs Moretti snapped back at him in Italian, and went on straightening the price lists. Then she opened up the hinged bit of the counter where you could pass through. She went up to Mr Moretti and held out her hand for the cup that he'd just finished drying. She spoke to him again and said something else in Italian, quieter now, but still a bit angry. You could tell from the way she reached up and banged the cup down on the shelf behind the sink.

Freddo caught my eye, a bit embarrassed, trying to see if I could understand what she was saying. I couldn't, though.

What was this all about? It was as if I'd stumbled into some big family argument, one that they'd had before, several times.

There was a bit of a silence after that. Mr Moretti smiled at me, winked, and went on wiping the cups. His wife took them from him one by one and lined them, more gently now, on the shelf.

Still nobody said anything.

Freddo shuffled his feet and glared at his mam and dad.

Aldo and me looked out at the street through the big glass window. There were little groups of people coming home from chapel, women mainly, black hymn books in their hands. Some kids dodged past them, running down the street to the station.

Finally, Mr Moretti dried the last of the cups and

handed it to his wife. 'You'd better get down the station,' he said, looking at Freddo. 'Or you'll miss the train.' He reached up to one of the shelves and took down a half-empty sweet jar. He unscrewed the top and handed us each a Minto. One each!

'Thank you, Mr Moretti!'

'Thank you, Papa!'

'Thanks, Dad!'

Freddo and Aldo threw their bathers on the counter and I left mine with theirs to pick up another time, and we tumbled out of the shop – quick – before the grown-ups could say anything else, each of us with a cheek full of Minto, sucking it slowly, enjoying it, determined to make it last as long as we could.

The station was just down the hill. In our village, everything was either up the hill or down the hill. Like most of the other places round here, all the houses and schools and chapels and churches were strung out in rows, one above the other, climbing up the steep sides of the valley.

Above them, on the valley tops, there was green open space, stretching for miles and miles. You could roam there as long as you liked with no one to tell you off, playing and having adventures.

And below, crammed into the narrow space on the floor of the valley was the Pit: the coal mine where most of our dads worked – when there wasn't a war on.

'Wasss the time now?' Freddo ran on ahead of us, dribbling sticky Minto juice down his chin.

I dribbled my reply. 'Nearly seven o'clock. Must be.'

'We going to be late?' puffed Aldo.

'Don't think so, Al,' I said. 'I didn't hear a train coming.'

We weren't late. They were. The evacuees.

There was a big crowd of people on the station platform. We could hear them before we could see them. When we got to the bottom of the hill where the bridge crossed over the railway tracks, the noise came funnelling up from below. It was just like our school yard at playtime.

We skidded to a halt on the bridge but Freddo and me were too titchy to see over the stone walls at the side.

'Give us a bunk up, Al,' said Freddo. 'Let's have a look.' Aldo grabbed his brother round the waist and lifted him up. He was a bit too keen though, so he nearly pushed him head first over the bridge wall.

'Oi! Take it easy, Al!'

Freddo wriggled free of his brother's big hands and held on tight to the edge.

'Sorry, Fred.' Aldo patted him on the back, making him cough. 'Do you want a bunk up too, Bob?'

'A'right,' I said, a bit nervous. 'But go easy, Al. Don't know your own strength, you don't.'

Very gently, he put both arms around my middle and lifted me up to hang from the stone wall. My knees got a bit grazed, but that was all.

Now we could see why there was such a noise coming from the platform. And why it sounded like our school yard.

It was packed with kids, running around, shouting, dodging in and out of the crowds. There were important people there too, giving each other orders: bigwigs from the Council, one or two of the chapel preachers, our teacher, Mr Rees. The scoutmaster marched up and down, barking something or other at some of the older boys.

'My dad told me the scouts were going to help carry the bags,' Freddo said. 'Come on! Let's go down.'

We jumped off the wall and ran across the bridge, me and Freddo bobbing up and down as we went, trying to get a better view. Aldo didn't have to. He was tall enough to see over the side, easy.

Stone steps led down from the bridge to the platform. At the bottom of the steps, near the little wooden waiting room, they'd set up some tables and on the tables were buckets filled with water. Women from the Ladies' Guild were bustling about, dipping mugs and cups into the buckets and setting them out in straight lines across the table tops.

'They'll be thirsty when they get here,' someone said. 'On the train all day in this heat. Poor things!'

'Hiya, Bob.' Ivor Ingrams pushed his way through the crowd with two of his mates. 'Where'd you go after Sunday School, butt?'

Ivor was in our class, mine and Freddo's. He always called everyone 'butt', short for 'butty'. That was our way of saying 'friend'.

He was good fun to play with, good at making up stories for us to act out. Bigger than us, too, which came in useful when we had battles to fight with the older boys. Only trouble with Ivor was that he sometimes got a bit spiteful about Aldo tagging along with us.

19

'We went swimming,' I told him.

'Of course. Should have known where the Pandy boys would be,' said Ivor. 'Why didn' you say, though, butt? We'd have come. Wouldn't we?' He turned to the boys standing at his shoulder, Billy Harris and Vic Thomas.

They nodded. 'What you eating?' Billy asked.

'Mintos,' said Freddo.

'My father gave them to us. For free!' said Aldo.

'Lucky!' said Vic.

The crowd was getting bigger now, more and more excited, wondering how long it would be until the evacuees arrived.

'How they going to decide who's going to live where?' asked Billy.

Gwenda Lewis was pushing her way past and overheard. 'They're going to take them to the school and sort them out there.' Gwenda was our age, but she went to the girls' school on the other side of the playground. She always knew the answer to everything. And *she* always carried her gas mask, in a cardboard box slung round her neck with string. Gwenda Gas Mask we called her, when we weren't calling her Miss Know-it-all.

'What you mean? Sort them out?' asked Billy.

'The people who said they'd take an evacuee . . .' said Gwenda, smug with knowledge, '. . . well, they've got to go to the school and choose who they'll take home with them.'

'Like a lucky dip,' Vic chipped in.

'What if nobody likes you?' Aldo asked sadly. 'Will they have to stay in the school for ever and ever?'

Ivor sniggered.

Quick as anything, Freddo came to his brother's defence, glaring defiance at Ivor. 'No, Al. They won't,' he told him. He was still sucking a bit of Minto, so he dribbled a bit when he said it.

'Mrs Chambers will sort it out,' Gwenda said. Mrs Chambers was the postmistress. She knew most things about most people in our village.

'Why her?' asked Ivor.

'She's the billeting officer. It's her job to make sure everyone gets a place to stay.'

The stationmaster came down the steps to the platform. He was only a little man – Mr Griffiths – but today he was puffed out with pride and self-importance. He was sweating too. He took off his peaked cap and wiped his shiny, damp forehead with a crumpled handkerchief. 'You children, behave yourselves,' he said, stuffing the hankie back in his pocket. 'Or I'll have to chuck you off the platform.'

He ran a finger round the inside brim of his cap to squeeze out the sweat.

'We're not doing anything, Mr Griffiths.' That was Billy.

'Well make sure you don't!' said Mr Griffiths, putting his cap back on and wiping his wet finger on his trousers. 'Or I will.' He headed off into the crowd.

Freddo called after him. 'Where's the train now, Mr Griffiths? How long's it going to be?'

21

Mr Griffiths turned and paused before he came up with his answer. 'Oh . . . about eight carriages and an engine,' he said. He thought he was a real wit.

'Ha, ha, ha!' we mocked, enjoying the joke really, but not wanting to admit it.

'Don't you know though?' Gwenda asked him. 'It's forty-five minutes late already.'

'It's at Blaenfelin,' said Mr Griffiths, marching off.

That was only two stops down the line. And as if to prove that it *was* nearly with us, that was the moment when we heard the train whistle echoing along the valley.

The excitement quickened as the news spread through the crowd. The scouts lined up and stood to attention. The councillors straightened their ties. The women from the Ladies' Guild slopped the last cups onto the tables.

Then, just minutes later, before we could even see the engine, we looked to where the railway lines came curving round the side of the hill and saw the thick clouds of grey smoke pumping into the air.

CHU-CHU-CHU! The sound of the engine bounced along the sides of the valley. CHU-CHU-CHU! it thundered, steaming closer now, as it struggled to haul its heavy load up the slope.

'They're coming!' someone shouted and people started clapping and cheering. 'The evacuees are coming!'

Chapter 3

Whooooooooooooooo!

With a long, deafening blast of the whistle, the black engine came steaming into the station, clanking and chugging, belching out its clouds of thick grey smoke. It was the longest train we'd ever seen, pulling eight or nine or ten carriages. We couldn't make out exactly how many because of the smoke, but we could see that they were painted green. Green carriages! Our carriages down here were brown and cream. This train was special. It had come from far away, somewhere different, exciting.

On the platform, the crowds began to cheer even louder. The women standing by the tables picked up their first mugs of water and got ready to hand them out. The important people made themselves look even more important, standing up tall, looking keen as mustard at the carriages drawing level with the platform.

Mrs Chambers, billeting officer, peered at the papers on her clipboard, beads of sweat dripping from her nose to smudge the inky writing.

At the platform edge, Mr Griffiths paced up and down, pretending to keep us kids in order. We went daft. All of us! Shouting and screaming, we ran along the platform, keeping pace with the train, dodging and diving through the smoke and the crowd. Aldo scattered people in his path as he charged along with us.

A screech of brakes, and a final long hiss of steam . . . and the train came to a stop.

Boys leaned out of the open carriage windows. More boys peered through the grimy glass of the windows next to the doors.

'They're all boys!' said Billy.

'The girls have gone to Pontfechan,' said Gwenda, Miss Know-it-all.

'I hope you never get captured by the Germans, Gwend,' said Ivor. 'You'd want to tell them everything. There wouldn't be any secrets left.'

Gwenda stuck her tongue out at him and ran back down the platform towards the end of the train. We followed, too excited to stay still.

'Stand away, there!' shouted Mr Griffiths. 'Let the poor blighters off!'

The carriage doors were opened, one by one, as we went skittling back along the platform, eyeing up the newcomers.

'Just a minute, boys!' A man standing in one of the open carriage doors leaned out and yelled to the kids in the train. A teacher, we reckoned. He had a teacher kind of voice. 'Wait until we tell you to disembark!'

Mrs Chambers wiped the sweat off her nose and scurried forward to talk to him. The women with water worked their way through the crowds and started pushing the mugs into outstretched hands.

Because the train was so long, some of the carriages at the back couldn't come level with the platform. The boys in these carriages shoved and pushed to hang out of the windows.

'Hiya!' we called.

'Hiya!' they shouted back. 'Where's this?'

'Tregwyn,' Vic said.

'Welsh Wales,' yelled one of the boys and the others in his carriage laughed.

They all looked a bit older than us, eleven or twelve maybe. Some of them had a school uniform on, so maybe they were in grammar school.

'You speak English!' one of them said, like as if he was surprised. 'Thought you only spoke Welsh down here.'

More laughter.

'Hey, mate!' A boy with red hair stretched his arm out of the window. 'Get us some water, will ya? Bleedin' hot in here!'

'*Cer i'w nôl e dy hunan, Cochyn!*' muttered Billy. 'There's Welsh for you!'

Those who could understand a bit of Welsh laughed at that. Under his breath, Billy translated it for the rest of us. '*Get it yourself, Ginger!*'

Then Aldo said, 'I'll get it.' Always ready to please was Aldo.

Before Freddo could stop him, he shuffled off down the platform into the throng.

'Mind how you go, Al,' his brother shouted after him.

'Who's the man talking to Mrs Chambers?' Gwenda asked the boys in the train.

'She that tall woman?' one of them said.

'Yes. She's the billeting officer. She works out where you're going to live.'

'Hope she puts me with you!' another boy yelled from two doors down.

We laughed then.

'No, you don't,' said Ivor. 'She'd be bossing you around all the time!'

Gwenda sniffed. 'Think you're funny, you do, Ivor Ingrams! My mam says we can't take anyone, anyway. It's all girls in our house and we haven't got a spare room.'

'Lucky!' whispered Vic.

'Who *is* he, then?' Gwenda pressed on. 'That man.'

'One of our teachers,' said the red-haired boy who'd asked for the water. 'Nobbsy!'

The boys laughed again. 'Mr Nobbs,' said one.

'Yeah. That's what I said. Nobbsy!'

They were all still laughing when Aldo came back along the platform, both hands cupped around a mug of water. He moved slowly, dodging the people jostling to and fro, concentrating hard on not letting any spill over.

'Well done, mate,' yelled the boy who'd asked for it. 'Hand it over then.'

'How's he goin' to do that?' Freddo asked.

The carriage wasn't anywhere near the end of the platform.

'We'll have to pass it along,' said Billy.

'Don't be daft,' said the boy. 'It'll get spilled. Or this thirsty lot will have drunk it all by the time it gets to me!'

'I'll fetch it to him, Fred,' said Aldo.

'How, Al? You'll have to go down on the side of the track.'

It was true. To reach the carriage, Aldo would have to walk down the sloping end of the platform and balance his way along the rough stones at the side of the train. Then he'd have to reach the mug up to the carriage window.

'If old Griffiths sees you, you'll be in dead trouble,' said Billy.

'Griffiths is too busy to notice,' said Ivor.

Further down the platform, boys were getting off the train now. With all the new arrivals, the crowd was busier and noisier than ever.

'Aw, come on mate,' called the boy in the train. 'I'm dying of thirst here. Be a pal, eh?'

'I can do it, Fred. Won't take a sec,' Aldo pleaded with his brother.

Freddo sighed. 'Go on then. But be careful, yes?'

Aldo slowly set off down the slope of the platform and onto the track bed, eyes fixed on the mug in his hands, careful not to spill a drop of the water. Big as he was, the train towered over him.

Some of the boys in the carriages whistled and cheered as he slowly picked his way over the uneven, stony surface.

'That's it, mate. Well done!' The boy shouted his encouragement as Aldo drew level with his carriage. He was nearly there, already beginning to reach the cup up to the open window, when one of the stones dislodged itself under his right foot.

Aldo stumbled, tried to keep his balance. The mug of water tipped in his hands and, before he could do anything to save it, it had poured itself onto the track bed.

Laughter and whistles and jeers and catcalls came tumbling out of the train. On the platform, Ivor cupped his mouth in his hands to hide his laughter. Billy and Vic turned away, pretending to look at the crowd behind them, but you could tell they were laughing too. Gwenda managed a pitying look, sort of.

The boy who'd asked for the water spat down at Aldo. 'You big, clumsy idiot. What'd you do that for? Can't you bleedin' 'old a cup, you nit?'

Freddo went tearing down the platform slope and stood at his brother's side, yelling up at the boy in the train. 'Don't you speak to him like that. Don't you *ever* speak to him like that. It was an accident! Right? *Right*?'

'OK, mate. Don't lose your rag! He's a bit clumsy, though, isn' he?'

'He was trying to help you!'

'Yeah, well. He didn't, did he? Bleedin' useless . . .' He turned away to mumble something to the other boys in his carriage. They laughed again and began pressing their faces to the grimy windows to mock Aldo.

He stood there, sad, but Freddo was even angrier than before. He jumped up to try and get hold of the door handle.

'Don't, Freddo,' I yelled. 'Don't be so *twp*! It's not worth it!'

'And they're all bigger than you!' added Gwenda.

Freddo wasn't listening though, and I honestly think

28

he'd have tried to open the door and pull the boy out of the carriage when a whistle blew and Mr Griffiths shouted, 'What's going on down there? Stand away, you children. The train's pulling up.'

All the other evacuees had got off the train by now, so they were going to move it forward to bring the last few coaches level with the platform.

Mr Griffiths came scurrying towards us and spotted Aldo and Freddo on the trackside.

'What on earth are you doing down there?' he shouted. He pointed at Aldo. 'Nothing he does would surprise me! But I thought you had more sense, Frederico. Get on this platform now!'

Freddo banged on the carriage door with his fist, before doing as he was told, shepherding his brother in front of him on the uneven ground. His face was like thunder.

Above them both, the evacuees peered down from the train. They were quiet now, but I could see some of them smirk and giggle as the two edged forward. The boy who'd asked for the water had disappeared inside the carriage.

'I warned you lot about misbehaving,' said Mr Griffiths. 'And now you have. Clear off home.'

'I haven't done anything, Mr Griffiths,' Gwenda simpered.

'Don't care!' said Mr Griffiths. 'You're mixing with them. So you can clear off too. Go on. All of you. Off you go!'

He turned to face the engine and blew his whistle for the train to pull forward.

Chapter 4

'Line up in twos!' The teacher from England was shouting at the boys on the platform. 'Come on. You know who your partner is.'

The evacuees shuffled into twos, dragging their belongings with them, calling out to each other. We thought they sounded funny, the way they spoke.

We ran back up the steps from the platform, Mr Griffiths shooing us away like a flock of mountain sheep. From the top of the steps, we watched the new arrivals finally shuffle into a long column. Other teachers marched up and down, pushing them into place, checking names on lists.

The women from the Ladies' Guild gave out the last of the water and Mr Griffiths took off his peaked cap, wiped his forehead and checked with Mrs Chambers that everyone was off the train.

Most of the evacuees had small suitcases, but some just had paper parcels bound with string. All of them had their gas masks, though, slung round their necks in cardboard boxes and they all had a label with their name on pinned to their jacket.

'Right! We're ready to go now,' shouted the teacher in charge. He'd been talking to Mrs Chambers. 'Follow this lady!'

Mrs Chambers started to climb the steps from the platform. Bright red and puffing, she came up onto the road where we were standing. The column of evacuees trailed behind her, kept in line by teachers, theirs and ours. People cheered as they passed.

'No trouble now, boys,' Mrs Chambers warned, panting as she came level with us.

'As if we would, Mrs Chambers,' Ivor teased.

'None of your cheek, Ivor Ingrams,' said Mr Rees, our teacher, as he passed by. He was helping to lead the way to the school where the evacuees would be sorted out and given their new homes. He stopped as the long line of boys straggled past. 'I saw what happened,' he said.

'Wasn't our fault, sir,' Gwenda chipped in.

'Don't care whose fault it was, Gwenda,' Mr Rees said. 'Don't want any more of it. These boys are a long way from home and we're going to look after them right. Understand?'

'Yes, sir,' we mumbled.

All except Freddo.

'Yes, Frederico?' Mr Rees leaned forward a bit, face to face with Freddo.

Freddo stared back at him. He was still wound up tight by his anger.

'Yes?' Mr Rees asked again, quiet.

The evacuees looked at us as they walked past. They were chatting and laughing. They didn't seem all that tired after their long journey, though some of them were a bit out of breath as they trudged on up the hill.

Mr Rees waited. 'Yes?'

'Yes!' You could hardly hear Freddo spit out his answer. 'But they'd better lay off Aldo!'

'I'm sure they will,' Mr Rees said, straightening up. 'Bet you'll all be best friends in no time at all. Team work tells, remember!' He joined the column again and walked uphill towards the school.

'I'm going home now,' said Billy.

'Me too,' said Vic.

'Are you having an evacuee?' Ivor asked them.

'Yes,' they said.

'And me,' I said. 'I bet my mam's gone up the school to get one.'

'See you tomorrow then,' said Billy, moving off.

'Yeah!' we said. 'See you!'

'Come on!' Ivor shouted to Billy and Vic, and sprinted up the hill. 'Let's be Spitfire pilots!'

And the three of them revved up their imaginary engines and took off through the streets, dodging and diving and gunning down enemy planes. Gwenda chased after them, gas mask bumping along behind, the string threatening to choke her.

Freddo was rubbing his hand, the one he'd used to bang on the carriage door.

'You all right now, Fred?' I asked.

'Yeah. I'm all right. But they'd better not say anything about Al!'

'Don't worry, Fred. I can look after myself.' His brother gave him a pat on the shoulder. 'I'm bigger than you. I'm not afraid of anything.'

'I know that, Al. That's what makes me worried! Come on. Let's go home.'

We split up at the top of the street and they went into their shop. The blinds were down because it would be blackout soon. Right from the start of the war, everyone had to black out their windows when it got dark, so no German planes would see the lights of houses and know where to drop their bombs. Not that that had happened to us – but people were still nervous that it could, one day. No street lights, either, so once it got dark, it was very, very dark.

My house was thirty-four doors down the street from the Morettis' shop, but I put on a burst of Spitfire speed too and was there in a flash.

My nanna called from the back kitchen as I spluttered in through the front door, another successful mission under my belt. 'Who's that?'

'Me, Nanna!'

'Where've you been, Robert? Your tea's been ready for hours.'

I went through the passage into the kitchen.

'Didn't Mam tell you I was going down the station to see the evacuees coming?'

Nanna was sitting in her big armchair by the fireplace. Her head was tilted towards the wireless that stood on the sideboard in amongst the empty fruit bowls and the vases and the picture of my dad.

She was small and dumpy, my nanna, and always wore a big flowery apron wrapped round her little body. She couldn't see very well now, so she spent a lot of time listening to the wireless. The voices were her friends, she said.

'Your mother's been running around like a mad thing, getting your room ready,' Nanna grumbled. 'Barely said "hello" to me, she has.'

I was going to have to share my bedroom with the evacuee.

'What's for supper, Nanna?'

'Carrot pie. It's in the oven.'

Carrots again! With the war, there wasn't always a lot of food to choose from.

I took the towel off the back of the kitchen door and used it to ease the pie dish from the oven. Someone had turned the gas off earlier so the dish wasn't very hot. I plonked it down on the big wooden table that took up most of the space in our kitchen.

I wasn't very hungry, really. I could still remember the taste of the Minto in my mouth. Sweet, lovely! 'You had yours, Nanna?' I said, taking knives and forks out of the table drawer.

'Oh aye,' she said, turning down the wireless. 'But if there's any going spare . . .' She eased her little round body out of the big chair, smoothed out her apron, and felt her way towards the table. Nanna was always ready for a bit of food.

We sat down together to eat and I shared out my helping of the stodgy, lukewarm pie. Nanna guided her fork carefully up to her mouth so as not to drop any food on the way.

'Wonder what Dad's got for tea?' I said.

My father was away, fighting in the Navy, somewhere in Norway. Narvik, my mam said, a place called Narvik. There'd been a lot of fighting there. We saw it on the newsreel when we went to the pictures. 'The battle of Narvik fjord' it was called, whatever a fjord was. A long stretch of water, like a lake, it looked, but

34

Freddo had told me that it was where the sea cut its way into the Norwegian coast.

Anyway, we all cheered when we saw our ships and planes giving the Germans what for, but when I looked at Mam in the smoky dark of the cinema, I could see that there were tears in her eyes. A lot of our troops had been pulled out of Narvik by now. I didn't know if Dad's ship was still there though. Or if he was still alive. We hadn't had a letter from him for ages.

'I don't know!' Nanna grunted as she fingered her plate to see if there was any food left on it. 'Why'd he have to go and join the Navy? He should have stayed down the pit!'

'He couldn't though, Nanna. He was called up, wasn't he?'

Like most men my dad's age, the order had come to join one of the armed services. He chose the Navy.

'It'll be lovely to see some sky,' he'd said to me the day he went away. 'I'll get some fresh air for a change, instead of being stuck down that black hole.'

Nanna licked her fingers, enjoying the last crumbs of carrot pie. 'Is it time for the blackout, Robert?' she asked. My nanna couldn't tell if it was dark outside or not.

'I think so, Nanna.'

'Do the curtains, then. There's a good boy. Don't want that Penry Lewis telling tales on us.'

Penry Lewis was Gwenda's father. He was an air-raid warden. He went round, making sure no light was showing. He could report you to the police if it was and you'd have to go to court and pay a fine.

I gave a last lick of my plate, cleared the table and set about doing the blackout.

Front-room windows were always done first. They were the ones you could see from the street. Then, upstairs. Next, the kitchen. Pin up the thick blankets on the window frame, check to make sure there were no gaps round the edges where the light could leak out, then draw the curtains. That's what you had to do.

'All done, Nanna.'

She was sitting back in her armchair now, one ear up close to the wireless. 'Good boy,' she said. 'Put the light on then, love, so you can see.'

We didn't have electric light in our house. We had gas instead. You had to turn on the gas to each lamp, and light the papery mantle with a match or a burning piece of paper.

I took my mam's matches from the sideboard drawer, and climbed up on a chair to see to the lamp over the kitchen table. Hisssss . . . went the gas and a pale, sickly, yellowish glow washed through the kitchen. It lit up the wallpaper with the leaf pattern and the brown wood of the doors and the zigzag shapes of the lino on the floor. I clambered down from the chair.

The front door banged open.

'Who's that?' shouted Nanna.

'It's me, Mam!' my mother called from the passage. She spoke to someone with her. 'Go on through. They're in the back kitchen.'

The front door closed and a figure came through the shadowy passage into the light.

'This is Reg,' my mother called out behind him. 'He's going to be staying with us for a while.'

It was the red-haired boy from the train.

The one who'd asked for the water.

Chapter 5

He was taller than me, sharp-eyed, hair slicked back with Brylcreem.

He had long trousers on and a white shirt and a blazer with a badge on the front pocket. He must have been older than me, then, in senior school. None of us had blazers and we always wore short trousers.

'This is Robert,' said my mother, nodding at me. She put the boy's case and gas mask down by the kitchen door.

'How d'you do?' he said, his eyes fixed on mine, daring me to tell what happened at the station. That's what I thought, anyway, but perhaps he hadn't even seen me in all that crowd.

'Hello!' I said.

Nanna turned off the wireless. 'Come here, boy. Let's have a look at you!' She swivelled her little body round to where she thought he was standing. She didn't quite look in the right place, though.

The boy looked at my mother, confused.

'Nanna can't see very well,' she whispered. 'You'll have to go right up to her.'

'Righty-o!' He crossed over to where Nanna was looking, put his face almost up to hers. 'Hello, Nan! How're you doing?'

She laughed. 'You're a cheeky one, you are. What's your name again?'

'Reg, Nan. Well, Reginald, really, but you can call me Reg!'

'Oh, thank you very much. I'm honoured.'

And they both laughed at that.

'A breath of fresh air, you are,' my nanna said, fumbling for his hand, giving it a pat. 'We need a bit of a laugh round here.'

He patted her hand back. 'You can count on me for that, Nan.'

My mother weaved her way round the table to fill the kettle at the kitchen tap. 'Would you like a cup of tea, Reg?'

'Ta. That'd be nice.'

'Sit down then. Make yourself at home.'

He sat down at the kitchen table, looking at me with the same dare in his eyes that I'd seen when he arrived.

'Robert,' said my mother. 'Don't just stand there. Make yourself useful. Take Reg's case upstairs.'

For a second, I hated her for making me do that. I lugged his battered brown case up to my bedroom and put it on the spare bed. Then I stood there in the dark, listening to the three of them laughing and chatting down in the kitchen.

There hadn't been much laughing in our house since my dad had gone away. Now, it felt like my mam was worried all the time. 'Worried sick,' she'd said to me once when I asked her how she was. She always seemed to be tired too, having to work all hours at the factory. My usually happy nanna caught her mood, sometimes. So did I, I suppose. We were all a bit edgy with each other, a bit short-tempered, and these days I never seemed to be able to do any good as far as my mother was concerned. Never mind. We'd all be as right as rain when Dad came back.

My mother called up the stairs. 'Robert! What are you doing now?'

'Nothing.'

'Come down and talk to Reg then.'

The thing was, you didn't really have to do much talking. Reg did most of it.

I sat, facing him across the kitchen table, jealous of the fact that my mam and nanna seemed to be lapping up every word he said.

Full of himself he was, cocky, confident, enjoying their attention.

He told us where he came from: Deal, in Kent. He said that it was at the seaside. That you could swim all day if you wanted. He was a bit of a champion swimmer, he said, except he hadn't done much swimming lately. Not since Hitler's armies had reached France, just across the English Channel from where he lived. Now the beach was off limits, all cordoned off with barbed wire and protected by explosives, in case the Germans should ever try to land there.

His dad was in the Army. He'd been fighting in France but he'd been brought home safe after the Germans had pushed the British troops back to the French coast. Our men had had to be rescued by a big fleet of boats.

His mam ('Ma' he called her), she worked in a factory, two bus rides away from Deal, doing important war work.

'Top secret,' he said. 'Can't tell you what it is! You might be spies. Enemy agents.'

Nanna nodded. 'Good boy. Careless talk costs lives!'

'Sometimes when she comes home, her skin's a sort of yellow colour. Get the picture?'

'Ammunition factory,' my mother said. 'It's working with the chemicals that does it. Like Phyllis Bevan, Mam.'

'Right,' Nanna said.

It was true that sometimes Mrs Bevan did look a bit yellow when she came home from the factory that made the bombs and shells.

Then Reg told us that when the Germans had pushed their way towards the French coast you could hear their guns booming away across the sea. Sometimes, even the houses in Deal shook. And there'd been German planes ('Dorniers' he said), just off the beach, dropping mines. Inland too, dropping bombs.

'Our anti-aircraft guns were going at it for over an hour,' he said, all dramatic.

'Anybody killed?' I asked. I didn't want to join in, but Reg was such a good storyteller that the words were out of my mouth before I could help myself.

'Naw,' he said, with a bit of a smirk, now he'd got me hooked.

He took a swig of tea. 'One of the bombs landed on a chicken farm. Killed all the cluckers. That's all!' He looked at me over the edge of the teacup, eyes staring straight at me, giving nothing away.

Was he having me on? I couldn't tell. He put his cup down, still looking at me. Straight-faced.

41

'Poor little chickens,' said Nanna.

'No eggs for breakfast next morning.' Reg laughed and the others joined in.

I didn't know if that story was true. I thought that maybe he'd made it up just to tease me. That he was laughing at me.

'So, anyway, that was when they thought it was time to move all the kids out.' He leaned back in his chair, rocking it to and fro on its back legs. 'Now old Hitler's in France, they reckon he's gonna try and invade us next.'

'The big bully!' Nanna muttered.

'Enough war talk,' said my mam, getting up from the table, clearing away the teacups. 'It's time for bed. I got work in the morning.'

My mother had a job in a factory that made wireless parts. Not Top Secret, though, like Reg's mother. 'And you got school, Robert.'

'We ain't,' said Reg. 'We just got to go and meet our teacher and find out what's going to happen to us next.'

'Is that Nobbsy?' I asked.

Reg's mouth was smiling but his eyes weren't. Now he knew for sure that I'd been at the station to see how he'd made a fool of Aldo.

'Yes. 'S'right, Mr Nobbs.' He stopped rocking in his chair and stood up too.

'The lavatory's out the back, if you need it,' said Mam, rinsing the cups under the cold-water tap.

'Outdoors?' said Reg, sounding a bit shocked.

'Yes.' My mam laughed. 'Take a bucket of water to

flush it with. And you can wash down here in the kitchen. In the bosh.'

'In the where?' Reg laughed.

'The bosh,' said Nanna, pointing. 'By there.' She could tell by the sound of the running water where my mother was. 'Where Myra's washing up.'

'Oh, the sink,' he said. 'You call it the bosh?'

'Yes,' said Nanna.

'Blimey. I'm not sure you do speak English after all!'

'Cheeky boy!' Nanna said, but she beamed with laughter as she said it.

Reg said goodnight to them both and headed for the passage. 'Come on then, Robert.' He put on a posh voice and called from the doorway, 'Show me to my room, old thing!'

Chapter 6

So Reg came to live with us.

And I'll tell you how it was. We shared my bedroom, but we didn't share anything else. We hardly spoke. He slept in the spare bed by the fireplace.

I made room for his things. I moved my jigsaws and my books and my Meccano set off the shelves next to the fireplace and shoved them under my bed; I put the little tin box with my collection of aircraft spotter cards there too.

He laughed when he saw what was in the box. 'Regular little Biggles, ain't ya?' (Biggles was a famous fighter pilot in books.) 'You want to collect comics, like me,' he went on. 'You'd get new cards every week.'

I pretended not to listen, and went on clearing space in the wardrobe and the chest of drawers, so that he'd have room for his clothes and his case and his precious collection of *Dandy* comics.

He never offered to show me them, ever. Didn't want to see them, anyway. Didn't want to have anything to do with him really, even though all the grown-ups told us to be pally, make the evacuees feel at home.

'He's missing his mam something shocking,' my mother said. 'He wouldn't tell you that, Robert, but he is. So you be nice now.'

My nanna thought he was great. He teased her all the time, made her laugh. 'I think you must be a secret agent, Nan, all the time you spend listening to that wireless. Listening out for coded messages, bet that's what you're up to.'

Sometimes she'd tell him off for being too cheeky. 'You think you're chocolate, you do,' she'd say, but she'd be laughing when she said it.

My mam thought he was a laugh too. Said he'd brought a bit of fun into our house, took our minds off worrying about my dad. Now and again, anyway.

He was extra polite to her, always clearing away his plate after we'd eaten, always going on about how she managed to make such tasty meals when sometimes there wasn't much food in the shops to choose from.

'Great turnip pie, Mrs Prosser. As good as me ma makes – and that's a compliment, believe you me.'

'Aw, there's nice,' said my mam and my nanna, both at the same time.

'You're missing her a lot, in't you?' my mam went on.

'Yep,' he said, and his voice got a bit choked when he said it. Then he caught my eye and he perked up and grinned at Mam. 'But I'm glad I landed up with you, Mrs Prosser. You're like a second ma, you are.'

'Aw,' she went again.

'There's lovely,' said Nanna.

Whenever they were around he pretended we were the best of friends. 'I'll let you see the sailor's cap my dad brought back from Dunkirk, Bob. When our lads got rescued. If you want.'

'There's a kind boy you are,' my nanna would tell him. 'What do you say, Robert?'

'Thank you,' I'd mutter through gritted teeth.

45

Didn't see much of him in the daytime, though, because the evacuees didn't go to school yet. No room for them, see. They wouldn't be going until the teachers could sort out where they could have their lessons. Gwenda Lewis said that soon we were going to have half-time school. We'd go in the mornings and the evacuees would go in the afternoons.

In the first few days after they came, though, they just met up with their teachers and spent their time playing games and walking about the hillsides.

And after school we never played with them. Which is why, up till now, Freddo had managed to stay out of Reg's way. He still had a grudge against him though. 'I hate that kid, honest. He's a right blummin' show-off!'

We were lying in the sun up on the hillside a few days after the evacuees had come. There were hardly any sounds up here, high above the village. From far below, on the bottom of the valley, we could just make out the clanking of the coal trucks being shunted in the pit yards.

Then the whistle blew for the afternoon shift and we watched the giant winding-wheel turning at the top of the mine shaft. It lowered the cage full of men down under the ground, into the darkness.

Freddo picked up a stone and threw it down the grassy slope. It was after school, and me and him and Aldo didn't feel like swimming today, so we'd come up here to play. We'd started with outlaws because Mr Moretti had taken the three of us to see the new *Robin Hood* film. (It was good going to the pictures with Mr

Moretti because he always brought a bag of sweets with him.)

Freddo and me took it in turns to be Robin. And when we weren't being Robin, we'd be the rich man who was going to be jumped on in Sherwood Forest. Aldo was always Friar Tuck.

Every time, the game would end with one of us being sat on by Aldo, pinned to the ground, breathless and wriggling, squirming to get free. Laughing.

'Aw, get off, Al!' one or other of us would yell. 'I can't blinkin' breathe.'

Whether it was me or Freddo playing the rich man, we'd always end up like this, flattened by Aldo, trying to topple him. Only way you could ever make him budge was to tickle him under the arm. Then Aldo would roll off, laughing and giggling and telling us to stop.

We'd got bored with that game today, though. Thought we'd have more fun being spies or fighter pilots, but it was so hot that we decided we'd have a bit of a rest first.

Which is why the three of us were sprawled out on the rough grass, squinting up at the empty, blue sky. Chatting we were, enjoying the warmth.

The talk came back to Reg again. 'Why did your mam choose him?' Aldo asked.

'Don't know, Al. Don't know if she had any choice. Anyway, she thinks he's great. And my nanna does.'

Freddo muttered, 'He'd better watch out is all I can say.'

'Where's he sleep, Bob?' Aldo propped himself up on one arm.

'In the spare bed in my room, Al.'

'Oh, right!' Aldo nodded, and then he carried on, 'Ivor Ingrams said their evacuee peed the bed.'

'I know,' I said.

'That's 'cos he's away from home and missing his mam and dad,' Aldo went on. 'That's what Mamma said, anyway.'

Freddo sat up and scowled. 'I'll go and pee in Reg's bed!'

I sat up then and the two of us looked at him, his face dead serious. Then he burst out laughing – and we did too.

All of a sudden, Aldo began to roll down the slope, scattering stones and bits of grass as he gathered speed. 'I'm a secret weapon,' he managed to shout back, still laughing. 'I'm going to roll down the village and crush Reg!'

'Yessssss! Yesssss! Yesssss!' Freddo jumped up and went whooping down the hillside after his brother. I got up too, keen to join in.

Then I saw a little group of boys puffing their way up the hillside towards us.

The evacuees. Nine or ten of them, with Reg leading the way, talking, making them laugh. In charge.

'Fred!' I yelled.

'What?' He hadn't seen them.

'Raiders approaching!' That was what we'd say if the air-raid sirens ever went off to warn us of enemy planes coming near.

Freddo stopped in his tracks and looked down at the little group.

'Get up, Al,' he almost barked at his brother.

Aldo, his shorts and shirt covered in dirt and grass, lumbered to his feet, unsteady.

The boys arrived and stood in a group with Reg in front, watching.

'Who's he supposed to be?' said Reg, pointing at Aldo, still bent over trying to keep his balance after his giddy roll down the hillside. 'Hunchback of bleedin' Notre Dame?'

His friends laughed.

'Leave him alone,' snarled Freddo. 'He's not doing you no harm.'

'A'right. A'right. Only joking. Can't you Welsh take a joke?'

'I'm not Welsh,' said Aldo. 'I'm Italian.'

'Shut up, Al,' whispered Freddo.

'Italian, eh?' Reg whistled.

'Eyeties!' One of the other boys sniggered.

'Your lot going to join the war then?' another boy piped up.

'Yes,' someone else chipped in. 'When Mussolini makes his mind up.'

'Mussolini?' Reg picked up on him. 'Mussoloony, you mean.'

They thought that was great. A couple of them patted him on the back. Mussolini was the Italian leader. He hadn't come into the war yet, and everyone was a bit edgy about whose side he'd choose if he ever did.

'Don't know anything about Mussolini,' Freddo

roared. 'We're Welsh, we are. I was born here, see. My Uncle Antony's in the RAF.'

'Gonna be a bit difficult for him if Musso decides to join in with Hitler then,' smirked Reg. 'He'll have to start attacking his own people.'

'He won't, will he, Fred?' Aldo was growing anxious.

Freddo started edging him away, down the hillside. 'It won't happen, Al. Don't worry!'

'Ain't you gonna stay and play?' asked Reg.

'No. Got to go for our tea,' Freddo said, almost in a whisper. He didn't want it to look like he was running away. I know he'd have liked to take Reg and the others on but he worked out there were too many of them for it to be a fair fight.

'Some other time, eh?' wheedled Reg.

'Yeah! Don' you worry!' Freddo marched on down the hill, fists clenched. Aldo loped along at his side, me following on.

Suddenly, Freddo stopped in his tracks and turned and smiled. 'Reinforcements,' he whispered to me under his breath and nodded down the hill.

Ivor and Vic and Billy were on their way up.

'Hey, Ive!' Freddo shouted. 'Come up here, butt! Reggie boy wants us to play with him and his friends.'

He turned to look round at the group of evacuees who had straggled down the slope to join us now. Freddo was smiling. I guess he'd reckoned that the six of us would be able to take on the English boys. After all, we had Aldo on our side and he'd make up for two or three others.

Ivor arrived, Vic and Billy in tow. 'What you gonna play, then?' he asked.

'Thought we could have a stone fight,' Reg said, stepping forward, cocky as ever. 'Take on the Eyeties.'

'Who're they, then?' Vic asked.

'Eye-ties?' said Reg, stretching out the word carefully. 'Don't you know?'

'Italians,' said one of the other boys. Ivor's evacuee, I think.

'Mussolini's lot,' said another.

'Thought we'd see what happens if Musso decided to finally join in the war,' said Reg. 'England v Italy. Fancy it, Ive?'

'He's Ivor to you,' snarled Freddo, almost beside himself now with rage at Reg's insults.

'And we're Welsh,' Aldo butted in. 'My mam said.'

Ivor sniggered.

'Shush, Al!' Freddo hissed at his brother.

'Course you are, mate,' Reg smirked. He winked at Ivor as he spoke. 'Course you are.'

Still looking at Ivor, he added, 'Welsh as a bleedin' ice-cream cornet.'

Ivor sniggered some more.

'I've got a better game,' Freddo jumped in, fed up with all this. 'Let's have a stone fight: England v *Wales*. Let's see who wins that one.'

He started edging in towards Reg, shoulders squared. Aldo edged forward too.

Freddo stopped, turned his head to where Ivor was standing. 'Come on, Ive,' he pleaded. 'Come on. Let's show this cocky swine that we won't take any more of his lip.'

He was close up to Reg now, standing as tall as he could to try and bring himself up to Reg's height. A few more steps and they'd be face to face, but Reg stood his ground. The other evacuees shuffled closer to him, but I could see that they were a bit nervous. Ivor's evacuee put his legs together and stuffed his hand down the front of his shorts.

'Come on!' Freddo edged even closer to Reg, faithful Aldo at his side.

I moved forward with them, nervous, excited, ready – sort of – to take on the English boys.

Ivor hung back. Vic and Billy shifted on the spot.

'Come on, Ive! Don't be windy!' Freddo urged.

But Ivor was looking at Reg, their eyes still laughing, enjoying making fun of Aldo. 'No. Don't fancy it,' he said. 'Got other things to do. Coming, Bill? Vic?'

And he turned away, quick as a flash, gathering speed with the other two as they raced off down the hillside.

Reg smirked some more. 'Can't rely on your mates these days, can yer?'

The other evacuees stepped up beside him to face the three of us.

In his rage, Freddo spat on the ground in front of them. Aldo copied him.

'*Diafol*,' Freddo snarled.

'What bleedin' language is that?' Reg laughed in Freddo's face. 'Eye-talian?'

'No, Welsh!' Freddo snapped back. He was shifting

around on his feet, frustrated, angry, ready to go off like a landmine.

But he knew this wasn't a fight we could take on. We all knew it. Not the three of us.

Freddo turned away, muttering. 'Just you wait! We'll get even!'

Reg laughed. 'Whenever you like, my friend.'

The brothers made off down the slope. The evacuees parted to let them go. I followed.

'You off as well, Robert?' asked Reg, all smarmy.

'Yes,' I shouted. 'I got to go home.'

'Say hello to Nan for me then.'

His mates laughed. They were still laughing as the three of us ran fast down the hill and, without a word, went our separate ways.

Too angry to speak, see.

And too ashamed.

Chapter 7

When Reg came in later and sat down at the kitchen table to eat with us, he didn't say anything about what had happened. I didn't either.

He teased Nanna. 'Any secret messages today, Nan, on that wireless of yours?'

He joked with my mam. 'Lovely fish pie, Mrs Prosser. Any fish in it?' He pretended that he and I were the best of friends. 'Let you read my comic later, Rob, if you want. Brought last week's *Dandy* with me. Good laugh it is. Got Addie and Hermann in it.'

That was Adolf Hitler, the German leader – and his sidekick Hermann Goering.

'Bet they'll be havin' Musso in it soon,' he went on. 'Can't wait.'

'Who?' said Nanna, sucking at her teeth to get at the last of the food.

'Mussolini, Nan. The Italian leader.' He looked at me as he said it.

'I know who Mussolini is, you cheeky boy,' said Nanna, laughing. She pulled a hankie out of her apron pocket and dabbed at her mouth. 'About time he made up his mind whose side he's on.'

'Looks to me like he's cosying up to Hitler,' said my mam, reaching across the table to collect the dishes.

'Looks like that to me too, Mrs Prosser,' Reg said, passing her his plate, nodding his head to agree with her, butter her up. He reached out for my plate. 'What do you reckon, Rob? You got some Italian mates, ain't ya? What do they think's gonna happen?'

'Dunno!' I muttered, handing my plate straight to my mother. 'We don't talk about it.'

'The Morettis *are* worried, though,' said Mam. She got up from the table to stack the dishes in the bosh. 'I was talking to Lena. If Italy goes in with Hitler, she doesn't know what will happen to the Italians living here.'

'Get rounded up, I expect,' Reg chipped in, still looking me in the eye. 'Interned. Like some of the Germans have been. They'll be enemy aliens, won't they, Rob?' He smirked at me across the table.

'Good heavens,' Nanna said. 'The Morettis are as Welsh as we are, now.'

'Yes,' Mam agreed. 'Been here long enough.'

'Lovely ice cream he makes,' said Nanna. 'Well, used to, before the war . . . before they started sugar rationing. Anything for afters, My?' (That was what Nanna called Mam sometimes, short for Myra.)

'No. Sorry,' my mother said, sitting back down at the table and lighting up a cigarette.

That set Nanna off on how many things had changed since the war started, so I got my *Boys' Own Paper* out of the sideboard drawer and started to read.

Reg said he'd go upstairs and write a letter to his mum and dad. He wanted to tell them how much he was missing them.

'Good boy,' said Nanna as he pushed his chair back under the table.

'They'll be missing you too,' said Mam.

'Oh, yeah, I know that,' he agreed. 'But I keep on telling them how lucky I am to be with you lot.' He winked at me as he went out of the kitchen. 'Landed on my feet, I have.'

And that's how it went on over the next few days. We avoided each other as much as we could and only talked to each other when we had to. When we were with my mam and my nanna.

At night, he got into his bed.

I got into my mine.

Neither of us said goodnight or anything.

In the daytime, when I'd go off to school, he'd meet up with the other evacuees and their teachers and they'd spend their time on their nature walks and playing games.

Then, after school, Freddo and Aldo and me made sure we stayed out of Reg's way. We'd go over the Pandy pool and swim and dive-bomb each other off the crane. Our new game was the British planes attacking German destroyers at the battle of Narvik.

'When is your papa coming back from there, Bob?' Aldo asked.

We were taking a breather, Aldo perched on the top of the crane. Before I could answer, he jumped, carrying a full stack of explosives, nearly flattening Freddo as he hit the water belly first.

BOOMPH!

The shock wave from Aldo's direct hit sent ripples of water up my nose and made me cough.

'BOOMPH! BOOMPH! BOOMPH!' went the echo round the rocky walls of the quarry.

'Haven't . . . heard . . . from . . . him . . . Al,' I spluttered. 'Don't . . . even . . . know . . . if he's still in . . . Norway.'

'Aw . . . don't choke, Bob. I'll come and give you a pat on the back.'

'No! . . . 'S'all right, Al! . . . Honest! . . . I'm OK . . .'

Freddo teased, 'He thinks you're going to squeeze his chest, Al. Like you did to Mrs Pritchard's cat.'

Aldo laughed.

We bobbed up and down in the cool water and splashed each other, shouting and hooting and firing our anti-aircraft guns full volume.

Then we tired of the battle and headed for the ledge and our cave.

That's when Freddo saw the others climbing down the rocky path.

'Bandits at three o'clock,' he warned.

It was Billy and Vic with Gwenda in tow. And some of the evacuees!

'What you playing?' someone shouted. It was Billy. He clambered across the stone blocks at the edge of the pool.

Freddo was on the defensive as we pulled ourselves out of the water. 'Nothing.'

I could see his eyes searching the group of evacuees, on the look-out for Reg. But Reg wasn't there.

That didn't surprise me. Once, when Nanna said that if he liked swimming he should go up the Pandy with us, he'd just said 'no thanks'. He said that he wouldn't

57

go near 'the piddly pool'. That's what he called it, to make Nanna laugh. From what he'd heard, it was too small and probably full of sheep droppings. 'Naw!' he'd said. 'The only place to swim is in the sea. Plenty of room to practise your strokes there.'

So, without Reg to lead them, this little bunch of evacuees had tagged along with Billy and Vic.

I suppose you could say some of them were getting on a bit better now with the village kids, even though others said us Welsh weren't very friendly. Sometimes, they said, we bullied them.

US, bully them? As if we would!

'We could hear you from miles away,' Gwenda piped up, scrambling the last few steps down the path, the others close behind. 'You wouldn't be any good as secret agents.'

'We weren't being secret agents,' Aldo said, shaking water off his hair like a big old dog. 'We were being fighter planes.' He flicked a few more drops in Gwenda's direction, then stopped, a bit dizzy.

One of the evacuees piped up, pointing at Aldo, 'How old is he?'

Freddo bristled. 'What's it to you?'

'He's a bit old for playing kids' games, ain't he?'

Aldo turned to his brother. 'I'm nearly sixteen, aren't I, Fred?' he asked.

'See what I mean,' said the boy.

Freddo stepped forward, struggling to keep his balance on the slippery stone blocks. Water dripped from his bathers.

'Mind what you say about my brother. Right?'

58

'Blimey!' The boy backed away a little, lost himself in the group. 'Keep your hair on!'

'Where's Ivor?' Freddo asked then.

Vic and Billy shuffled their feet and looked at the water. 'Dunno,' said Vic.

'I do!' said Gwenda, Miss Know-it-all.

'Shut up, Gwend,' said Billy.

'Why should I? He's gone off with his evacuee.'

'The peeing boy?' said Aldo.

Everyone laughed at that, even the evacuees.

'And a new friend!' Gwenda again. 'You'll never guess who?'

But I knew; so did Freddo.

'Reg!' We spat his name out at the same time.

'He's a blummin' traitor, that Ivor Ingrams!' Freddo almost choked out the words.

Billy and Vic sort of agreed, not too loudly though, because one day Ivor might want to be friends with them again.

'When did they get to be friends, then?' I needed to know.

'He went round Ivor's house to see Ivor's evacuee,' Vic said.

'Then Reg showed Ivor his aircraft spotter cards,' said Billy.

'Reg hasn't got any,' I said.

Billy shrugged. 'Ivor has, though. He said that Reg told him that he tried to swap with *you*. But you weren't interested.'

'He's lying! He doesn't collect spotter cards.'

'You do, Bob,' said Aldo.

'Yes, Al.'

'*Did*, more like,' one of the evacuees said to his mates. They sniggered.

I felt my face flare red with anger. 'I'm going home!' I said. 'You coming, Fred?'

'Yes.' He turned back to the cave where we'd left our clothes. 'Come on, Al. Let's dry off.'

Gwenda followed us, came to the mouth of the cave. 'What are you going to do to Reg, then?' Her voice echoed from the dark walls.

'Dunno,' I muttered, pulling my shorts on over my bathers.

'Nothing, I expect. He's bigger than you!' said Gwenda.

I didn't say anything to that, but my eyes began to smart.

'He's crying,' said one of the evacuees. They'd traipsed after Gwenda and gathered by the cave, peering in.

'I'm not!' I bent down to pick up my daps, turning my face away from the light. 'I'm not crying.'

'Yes, you are,' said Aldo, struggling into his own daps. 'Why you crying, Bob?'

I told him. 'Because I'm angry, Al.'

'Because you're scared, more like,' another evacuee piped up.

'No, I'm not.'

'Come on. Let's go!' Freddo butted in, shepherding Aldo, half dressed, out of the cave.

Gwenda and the others stood aside to let us pass.

'I'll get even, don't you worry,' I shouted back as we

clambered up the stone blocks from the water's edge. 'I'll show him!'

The little group of evacuees gave a cheer – but it was a mocking cheer, one that said that I couldn't do anything, that I wouldn't ever be able to get the better of Reg.

I was afraid that they were right.

Chapter 8

Slam! I banged the front door shut and charged upstairs to my bedroom. My bathers were still damp under my shorts, but I didn't care.

'What on earth's going on?' Nanna yelled from the back kitchen. 'Who's that?'

'Me, Nanna!' I could hardly speak, I was so choked up with rage.

'What you doing, Robert?'

'Nothing!' I shouted down to her.

The bedroom looked like I'd left it that morning, my stuff piled up by the side of my bed, Reg's piled up by his.

'I'm looking for something, Nanna. That's all.' I went down on my hands and knees and wriggled my way underneath the bed.

The late afternoon sun was slanting in through the window, but most of the room was in shadow and it was dark under the bed. Dust got up my nose and made me sneeze, but I rooted around in the jumble of books and toys and games, looking for the little tin box where I kept my aircraft spotter cards.

My grampa had brought the box back from when he was a soldier in the Great War. That was long before I was born, but Nanna had kept it and given it to me for my birthday one year. 'For keeping precious things in, Robert.'

With Reg sharing my room, I'd pushed it right up against the wall, under a pile of books. No safer there than anywhere else in the room, I knew that, but I wanted to keep it from Reg's prying eyes.

I fumbled my way to where I knew the box should be. My hands closed round it and I wriggled my dusty way back out from under the bed.

I sat on the floor and opened the box.

Empty!

No cards! I knew there wouldn't be. I knew! I banged my fists on the hard bedroom floor, shouting, tears coming hot and fast now.

'What you doing, Robert?' It was Nanna again, calling up from the kitchen.

'He's stolen my cards, the swine!'

'Language!' Nanna scolded. I could hear her feeling her way along the passage downstairs. 'Who's stolen what?'

'My spotter cards. He's taken them and given them to Ivor Ingrams.' I got to my feet and went, sobbing, to the landing.

Nanna stood in the passage, face turned upwards, not seeing. 'Reginald wouldn't do a thing like that.'

'Yes, he would. He HAS!'

'Have you looked everywhere?'

'I don't need to. I always keep them in my box. And they're . . . not . . . there . . . any . . . more!' I wasn't crying now, but I could hardly choke my words out.

'Oh well,' said Nanna. 'Wait till Reg gets home and I'm sure he'll help you look!'

'You think he's great, you do!' I screamed downstairs. 'You think he can't do anything wrong! Ever.'

'Don't you speak to me like that, my boy!' Nanna was shouting now. 'I'm your grandmother but I get more respect from Reginald than I do from you these days.'

'He doesn't respect you, Nanna. He's laughing at you – only you can't see it!'

'There's nasty you've turned, Robert. If I had my sight, I'd be up there to give you a good slap!'

'What's all this about, then?' Mam stood at the open front door. 'What's going on?'

'He's been giving me cheek, Myra.'

'So I heard. What about?'

I leaned over the banisters so I could see my mother better.

'Reg stole my cards. My spotter cards.' I was still choking with anger.

'He doesn't know for sure, Myra,' Nanna said. 'He hasn't looked properly.'

'Have you?' Mam asked.

'What?'

'Have you looked in your bedroom properly?'

'I don't have to. I know he's taken them.'

'Come down here!'

'No!'

'Come here, Robert. Because if you don't, I'll come up there and give you such a hiding!'

'He's gone too cheeky for words, My.' Nanna turned and shuffled along the passage into the back kitchen. 'Jealous, he is!'

My mam called upstairs again. 'Are you going to come down? Yes or no?'

'Yes.'

'Come on then. I'm tired. I've been working a double shift. I don't want to stand here all day.'

I started down the stairs. Slowly. I was afraid of my mother's temper and I couldn't work out how angry she was now. I might really get a good hiding.

I didn't though, because Reg saved me from it. He came through the front door, large as life, his usual cocky self.

'Wotcha?'

'Hello, Reg,' my mother said.

'You look tired, Mrs Prosser.'

'Yes, I am, love. And Robert isn't helping.'

He looked up at where I was standing, halfway down the stairs. 'What's up then, butt?' The usual smirk, the smiling, knowing eyes. And he called me 'butt'. Who did he learn that off?

Nanna called from the kitchen, 'Is that you, Reg?'

'It is, Nan,' he shouted back. 'Picked up any coded messages today on that wireless of yours?'

She laughed, as usual.

I stood there, sulking, hating him. Hating them, too, for being taken in by his charm.

'What seems to be the problem, Rob?' He made it sound like he was really concerned.

'My cards have gone. My spotter cards.'

'Bad luck, butt. Where've you left them, do you think?'

'I haven't left them anywhere.'

'So where are they then?'

'*You* know!'

'Well, sorry, but I don't. I'll help you look for them, though. Excuse me, Mrs Prosser.' He did a neat side-swerve past my mam and me, bounding up the stairs, two at a time.

I went to follow him, but my mother stopped me. 'No more of this nonsense, now, Robert,' she hissed. 'You learn to get along better with Reg. Right?'

I didn't say anything, but I could feel tears coming back. It wasn't fair. It seemed to me they were always ready to cosy up to him, take his side.

'Well?' Mam whispered.

'Yes,' I mumbled, not wanting to say any more because I couldn't trust myself not to cry.

From the bedroom came the sounds of stuff being moved around, and then Reg called out in triumph, 'Found 'em!'

I raced upstairs, Mam following.

Reg stood by my bed with the blankets thrown back and the pillow on the floor. In his hand, he held a stack of cards. 'This what you been looking for, mate?'

'Where were they, Reg,' my mother asked, shaking her head as if to say how stupid I was.

'You'd tucked them under your pillow, Rob.'

'No, I didn't.'

'Must have been looking at them before you dropped off last night.'

'No, I wasn't. You put them there, now. When you ran upstairs.'

I knew he had. Of course he had.

'That's enough, Robert,' my mother chipped in. 'Let's stop all this nonsense now. You've got your cards back. So, apologise to Reg and come and help me make the tea.'

'Apologise for what?'

'For saying he took them.'

'You didn't say that, did you, Rob?' Reg laid the cards on the bed and put on a big show of looking shocked. 'Why'd you say that?'

'Because you took them to show to Ivor Ingrams.'

'Got it wrong there, mate. Whoever told you that? I was showing Ive . . .'

'Ivor,' I muttered.

'. . . I was showing my butty Ivor *my* football cards. My dad's they are, really. See!'

And like a flash magician on the stage, he pulled a set of cards from his trouser pocket and fanned them out for us to look at.

I knew he was lying. I knew he'd taken my cards to get Ivor to be his friend. He may have given some away for all I could tell. I wasn't going to cry any more. I was angry now, raging inside.

'Say "sorry",' my mother prompted. 'Go on!'

Reg looked at me, the same sharp, smiling eyes, the same smirk.

'Robert!' my mother said. 'I'm waiting! And I won't wait much longer.'

I had never felt so miserable in all my life.

In the dark, shadowy bedroom, with my mother and Reg watching and waiting for the word that would choke me to say, all I wanted to do was curl up in the bed and wish everything away.

I wished there wasn't a war.

I wished that my dad was home.

I wished that boy had never come.

'Sorry,' I said.

Chapter 9

'SORRY!'

Freddo went off like an exploding shell. 'YOU SAID SORRY?'

He banged his fist down so hard that black ink slopped out of the inkwell and ran across the top of our desk. It was the next morning. School time.

Mr Rees looked up from his table at the front of the classroom. He was listening to Trevor Davies reading out loud.

'What's going on, Frederico?'

'Nothing, sir, an accident, that's all.'

Mr Rees went on listening to Trevor.

Ivor had turned round, though, to see what was happening.

I stuck my tongue out at him and he went back to his work, smiling.

'Why d'you do it?' Freddo whispered now, still angry. 'Why d'you apologise to HIM!'

'My mam made me.'

'But he took your cards, didn't he?'

'Yes. I think so.'

'What do you mean?'

'There were none missing when I counted them afterwards. I think he took them to show off to Ivor. To show he could take them if he wanted to. That he could do anything he liked.'

'Stop talking, Robert Prosser!' Mr Rees called out without even looking up from the book Trevor was reading to him. 'And, the pair of you, get on with your work.'

'Yes, sir!'

'Sir!'

And that's how we left it. We didn't really have a chance to talk to each other until it was time to go home for dinner. We were only having morning lessons now. The evacuees took over our classroom for the afternoon.

We jostled our way through the BOYS doorway, shouting and ragging and racing to be free for another afternoon of sun.

'Coming over the Pandy?' Ivor passed by, head high above the crowd.

'With you?' I said. 'No thanks!'

'Thought you'd be waiting for your new friend,' Freddo joined in. 'See if he's pinched someone else's cards.'

'Don't know what you're talking about,' Ivor bounced back. 'You coming, Vic?'

Vic looked at us, doubtful, wavering. 'If Billy comes, yeah.'

'Coming, Bill?' Ivor asked.

Billy deliberately didn't look at us, didn't hesitate. 'Why not!'

'Come on then.' Ivor ran on ahead, calling back to us as he went. 'Go and get your bathers and I'll see you up by the cave.' He stopped in the middle of the jostling boys and looked at us. 'It'll be a'right if you change

70

your mind and come up later. We're not fussy who we play with, are we, Bill?'

He turned and ran off.

'No,' said Billy, trying to catch up with him. 'What'll we play, Ive?'

'What about playing traitors?' Freddo shouted after them as they scooted off down the street. But they just laughed and went on running, only swerving down a back alley to avoid Gwenda coming out of the GIRLS entrance.

We swerved as well, into the front door of the Wool Shop. Gwenda passed by, chopsing, talking at top speed, telling her friends how her father had reported someone for letting light show through their blackout curtains.

'. . . they could have been sending signals to enemy planes . . .'

It was true that we were hearing more German planes overhead these nights.

Gwenda rattled on, fainter now, '. . . and Mr Spinetti from over Deri had to go to court for having a revolver hidden under his floor-boards . . .'

'That's my uncle,' Freddo whispered. 'I didn't know!'

A shadow suddenly blocked out the sun. 'What you two doing here?' It was Aldo coming to meet us from school. 'Have you been buying wool, Bob?'

'I haven't, Al,' I laughed. 'We were taking shelter from Gwenda – but I think we've got the All Clear now.' That was the siren that went off when enemy planes had flown away overhead.

'Raiders passed!' said Aldo.

'Yes, Al,' said Freddo.

71

We shuffled out of the doorway, keeping an eye on Gwenda in the distance, still talking, and walked down the hill to the café.

The evacuees were coming up on the other pavement with Mr Nobbs, their teacher, on their way to school. A couple of them shouted over the road to us. 'Hiya!'

'Been keeping our seats warm, have you?'

'Got any spotter cards, mate?'

That was Reg, walking jaunty as you like, on the edge of the group, balancing on the kerb.

A couple of the others laughed, in the know.

'Come on,' said their teacher. 'Stop wasting time.'

And they straggled past, up the hill, Reg holding court, telling them, I bet, about how he'd taken my cards. ('Just borrowed 'em,' he'd have said. 'Just for a laugh.')

'What they talking about, Bob?' Aldo asked.

'Nothing, Al. Don't worry.' I changed the subject. 'What we going to do this afternoon, then? After dinner?'

'Go swimming?' Aldo was eager.

'Ivor and that lot have gone over the Pandy, Al,' Freddo said. 'And we're not friends with him, remember?'

'Yes. He let you down, didn't he, Fred?'

'Yes, he did, Al. Wouldn't take our side, would he? Against Reg?'

'No.'

We walked on in silence for a bit, Aldo jumping on and off the edge of the pavement, thinking hard. 'I could dive-bomb him off the crane.'

72

We laughed. 'No one deserves that, Al,' said Freddo. 'Still, we shouldn't let Ivor Ingrams, or anyone else . . .'

'. . . Like Reg!' Aldo chipped in.

'. . . Like Reg!' Freddo carried on. 'We shouldn't let anyone else stop us doing what we want to, should we?'

'No!' me and Al shouted. 'NO!'

I dodged out of the way, sharpish, as Aldo stopped his kerb jumping and tried to give me a pat on the back.

'So if we want to go swimming . . .' Freddo broke into a run then, stretched out his arms to make wings, and shouted, '. . . if we want to go swimming . . . we'll go swimming.'

'YES!' Aldo and I were shouting too, spreading our wings, taking off. 'YES!'

The three of us powered up our engines and flew. We swerved and pitched and roared down the hill, to glide to a safe landing on the doorstep of Moretti's café.

Mr Moretti was outside with a bucket of water and a cloth, cleaning the shop windows. 'Hello, boys. Successful mission, was it?'

'Yes, Papa,' Aldo puffed, jiggling about a bit as his propeller wound down. 'No losses.'

'Your Uncle Antony would be proud of you boys,' said Mr Moretti, smiling. Then he asked if there was any news of my dad and I said there wasn't.

'Sorry to hear that, young Roberto,' he said and went on wiping down the windows. 'So what are you three up to this afternoon?'

'Don' know, Dad,' Freddo said.

'Not going up the Pandy?'

'No, Dad. Maybe we'll go up the mountain.'

'Very good,' said Mr Moretti, wringing out his cloth and picking up the bucket. 'Don't forget your bathers, then.' Still smiling, he gave us a big wink and went into the shop.

'See you after dinner, Bob,' Freddo said, laughing, following his dad inside.

'Bring your bathers,' said Aldo, joining him. 'Like Papa said.'

'All right,' I said. Though I wasn't looking forward to being with Ivor and that lot very much, to tell the truth.

Still, Reg wouldn't be there. For once. We could maybe all play together again. Like we did before the evacuees came.

Except that it wasn't that easy to get away from Reg.

As we found out.

Chapter 10

The three of us had turned up at the Pandy pool, bathers already on under our shorts.

'*Duw, duw*. Look who's here!' yelled Ivor, his voice echoing around the flat chiselled stones of the quarry . . .'

Billy chipped in: 'Didn't expect to see you.'

The two of them were with Vic, splashing around, climbing up the crane head, jumping off, whooping.

'Haven't come to play with you lot,' Freddo shouted back as we clambered over the stone blocks to our cave at the water's edge.

'We've come for a swim,' said Aldo, backing up his brother. He pulled his shorts down over his swimming trunks, took off his shirt and daps and bundled them into the cave where the others had left their stuff too. He stood on one of the stone blocks, ready to dive into the cool, dark water.

'Watch out, boys!' Ivor warned. 'Big wave coming.'

'Leave it alone, will you?' Freddo snarled.

Aldo hesitated, half crouched like he was going to dive, but not sure how this was going to go.

'Aw, come on, Freddo. 'S'only a joke.' This was Vic, calling out, trying to make the peace.

Freddo wasn't having any of it. 'He's always joking about Al,' he shouted back.

'It's just jokes, though. Innit, Ive?' Vic again.

'Yes. Course!' Ivor said, hanging off the crane, looking straight at Freddo across the water. 'Can't you take a joke, butt?'

He slipped down into the water, but as it closed over his head, I could see he was smiling. Smirking, really.

Freddo hadn't noticed, I think, because when Ivor came to the surface again, spluttering and shaking the water from out of his eyes, Freddo said, 'Well, just lay off it, will you? It's not funny.'

'A'right! A'right!' said Ivor and he swam towards us on the bank. Vic and Billy swam after him, at a bit of a distance, though, in case things turned ugly and Freddo's temper got the better of him. Aldo had straightened up by now, and stood looking at his brother, not knowing what to do.

Ivor and the others swam a bit nearer, just a bit, though.

'Still haven't forgiven you lot for not taking Reg on,' Freddo said. 'So don't think you can smooth things over that easy.'

Ivor had reached the edge of the pool. He looked up at us, treading water. 'We couldn't have taken that lot on, Freddo.'

'We could have!'

'No, we couldn't. Don't be daft! There were too many of them.'

Aldo joined in. 'You and me could have handled the little ones, Ive.'

'Oh, that's a good one, Al,' Ivor sneered. 'That would have left Freddo and Bob to take on Reg and all the rest of them.'

Billy came doggy-paddling up to the water's edge. 'Oi. We were there as well.'

'Oh, aye,' said Ivor. 'Two half-pinters like you would have made a lot of difference.'

Billy opened his mouth to protest, but thought better of it. Or maybe he realised there was maybe some truth in what Ivor was saying.

'You going to play, then?' Ivor asked us now.

'Play what?' Freddo asked, not keen, but thawing out a bit towards Ivor. He turned away into the cave and took off his shorts and shirt.

'Battle of Narvik fjord?' Ivor yelled after him. 'You lot like playing that, don't you? You can be the RAF and dive-bomb us. We'll be the German fleet.'

'Robert's papa was there,' Aldo said.

Ivor turned his head to where Vic and Billy were treading water. '*Papa!*' he mouthed, silently, smirking again. '*Papa.*'

They bobbed down under the water, giggling.

Freddo, still in the cave, didn't see.

'He was, wasn't he, Bob?' Aldo went on, not knowing that they were laughing at him.

'Yes, Al.' I didn't want to talk about it. Not with Ivor there, mocking. Sly, he was. I thought that more and more.

Vic and Billy came up to the surface again, straight faces now. Freddo shot out of the cave and jumped into the water, body rounded into a ball. I stripped down to my bathers.

Aldo went on, 'But you don't know where your papa is now, do you, Bob?'

'No, Al.'

The others went a bit quiet, till Billy chipped in, 'No news is good news, Bob.'

'Yes. S'pose so.' I jumped into the water, deep down into the cool blackness of the pool. Above me I could feel the shockwave of Aldo hitting the water and the others thrashing around and shouting.

I didn't know where my dad was, that's true, and I wanted him back. But all you could do was wait, and if you went to chapel, you could pray.

We didn't pray in our family, not even Nanna. So what Billy said was true enough: no news was good news.

Because we'd have heard from the War Office if he'd been killed. We'd have had the telegram saying he'd been lost in action. Like Mrs Field, three doors up, whose son had been killed in France.

I kicked up to the surface and choked out, 'Why did Reg bring you my spotter cards?'

Ivor swam up to me. 'I dunno, butt. I didn't even know they were yours. Got 'em back, didn't you?'

'Yes.'

Reg obviously hadn't wasted time boasting about how he'd managed to slip them back into my bedroom.

'There you are then,' Ivor said. 'No harm done.'

'Why'd you make friends with him, though?' Freddo asked, swimming around us.

'He's not a real friend,' said Ivor.

'Looks like he is.'

'No, he's not. I know who my real friends are, don't I?'

'We are, Ive, aren't we?' queried Aldo. 'We're your real friends.'

'Course you are, butt.' Ivor swam away from us, calling over his shoulder, 'Come on, let's pick sides and get the game started.'

Freddo shouted to his retreating back, 'Let's play something different. Fed up with Narvik fjord.' He caught my eye as he swam up at my side. 'Aren't *you*, Bob?'

'Yes,' I said, treading water. 'Let's play something different.'

'What, then?' Ivor yelled, flipping onto his back, floating.

'Convoys and U-boats!' Billy dog-paddled up to us.

'Oh, yes! And I'll be a U-boat.' Aldo ducked underwater and slid away towards the crane, a human torpedo. He came up, thrashing the water, triumphant. 'See! I can stay under longer than anyone!'

'A'right, then,' said Ivor. He swam back towards us. 'Bob and Billy and Vic can be the convoy and me and Freddo'll be the escort. What d'you say, Fred?'

'A'right,' Freddo muttered, still a bit reluctant.

'Let's get started then.' Ivor was back with us now, giving orders. 'You three set sail and we'll protect you from the U-boat. Right, Al. You got to try and get through our defences.'

So that's what we played, taking it in turns after a while to be the U-boat so we didn't have Al jumping on us all the time and pulling us under the water. No one was as good as him, though.

I suppose we'd been playing for about an hour, when Vic and Billy finally said they'd had enough and struggled out of the pool and onto the rocky lip of the cave. Freddo and Ivor and me were their escort, getting them safely to shore. Aldo stayed on the crane, climbing to the top, crashing back into the water, shouting, whooping, in a game of his own now.

We lay out in the sun, friends again, in a way.

'Raiders!' Aldo's voice echoed across the water.

'Where, Al?' Freddo and the rest of us sat up, heads scanning the quarry walls.

'By there, look!' Aldo pointed up the path that led down to the pool.

Two of the evacuees were clambering down the ledges, waving, shouting, but from where we were, we couldn't hear what they were saying.

Ivor jumped up, a puddle forming around his feet. 'It's Norman,' he said.

'Your evacuee?' said Billy.

'Yes. What's up, I wonder?'

Freddo winked at me as he got to his feet. 'Maybe he's peed himself again.'

'It's not funny, Freddo.' Ivor came to his evacuee's defence. 'He can't help it.'

'Well, there you are then. Now you know what it's like when you make fun of Al.'

'Who's making fun of me?' Aldo came swimming, strong and powerful, up to the water's edge.

'No one, Al. Don't worry,' said his brother as Aldo beached himself on the warm rock in front of the cave. We were all on our feet now, looking at the two figures racing closer.

'They're making a heck of a fuss,' Billy said. 'Wonder what's happened?'

'Perhaps the war's over,' said Aldo.

'Great!' I said. 'Then Reg and his friends can all go back to England!'

The boy called Norman was nearly with us now.

'What's up, butt?' Ivor called. 'What's the matter?'

'There's a parachutist come down on that big common.' He meant Maesgwyn Common, a mile away up the hill.

The two boys skidded to a stop, breathless, excited. 'He's caught in a tree!'

'Where you going, then?' Freddo asked.

'To tell the police. Like you're supposed to.'

There was a lot of talk, these days, about the threat of enemy airmen invading us by dropping from German planes by parachute. People said they might come in disguise, as nuns or priests or nurses, maybe. Everyone had to be on the look-out and if you spotted one you had to tell the police straightaway.

'Who spotted him then?'

Norman took a deep breath and made as if to set off again. 'Reg did. We went up there after school.'

Trust Reg!

'Let's go and have a look.' Ivor started scrabbling around for his clothes, the others too. I hesitated.

'In't you coming, Bob?' Freddo balanced on one foot as he struggled to get his shorts on.

Part of me wanted nothing to do with it, if Reg was involved. But another part of me wanted the excitement of seeing the parachutist captured. That part won.

'You bet, Fred!'

Chapter 11

The two evacuees went panting off to the village and the six of us got dressed quick and scrambled up the quarry sides. Then we set off along the path to Maesgwyn Common. We whirled our wet bathers round our heads, spraying each other as we raced along.

'Tell Mr Richards!' Freddo turned round to run backwards, and shout to the disappearing evacuees.

'Who's that?' they shouted back.

'Our bobby,' Vic yelled, not bothering to look back. 'PC Richards.'

'And Penry Lewis,' Ivor added, running backwards too, side by side with Freddo. 'ARP warden.'

'Oh no, Ive,' Billy wailed. 'Then Gwenda will turn up.'

'She'll turn up anyway,' Freddo panted, charging on. 'She's got built-in radar, she has.'

The path from the Pandy pool climbed way up the hillside before flattening out on the big, open common. It was scrubby land, gorse and ferns and whinberry bushes mostly, with rocks and small trees dotted here and there. By the time we were near the top of the slope, we were red faced and puffing like steam trains.

'Hang on,' panted Freddo as we reached the edge of the common. 'Better not show ourselves, straight off. Don't know where this parachutist is.'

'Or if he's got a rifle!' Billy dropped to the ground like a stone. The rest of us followed, sharpish.

'One of us had better creep up and have a look then,' Ivor said. 'See if we can spot him.'

'And Reg,' said Vic.

'I'll go,' Aldo volunteered and was halfway on his feet before Freddo pulled him down.

'No, Al. You're too big. They'll see you.'

'I'll make myself small, Freddo. Like a cat.'

'Like Mrs Pritchard's cat?' Ivor smirked, winking at Vic and Billy.

'Lay off, Ivor,' Freddo snarled. 'You can't leave it alone, can you?'

'A'right. Don't get shirty!' Ivor said. 'But it's true, Al. We should send someone smaller to take a look.'

'Like Billy or Vic, like?' Aldo was being helpful, but I don't think either of them was too happy with his suggestion.

'Or Bob!' Vic protested.

Billy chipped in. 'Yeah. He's not much bigger than us.'

'A'right,' I said. 'I don't mind.' I left my rolled-up bathers on a rock and edged forward on my belly over the rough ground. Ferns and gorse tickled and scratched through my shirt, but I didn't care. I was an ace commando now on a secret mission to smash the spy ring – just like in the films.

'See anything, Bob?' A radio message came crackling through from base. Freddo!

'Not yet,' I radioed back. 'Roger and out!'

'He's playing secret agents,' I heard Aldo whisper loudly to his brother.

'Yeah. Shush, Al.'

I edged forward a bit more. I was on the lip of the hill now. Camouflaged by ferns, the common spread out in front of me. No sign of a parachute anywhere. No sign of Reg and his mates. In the distance, a train chuffed its way down the valley, grey smoke trailing into the sky.

Then a little breeze ruffled the ferns, and away to the left, something white flapped in the trees.

'Alien object at ten o'clock. I can see it!' I radioed back to the command post.

'Is it a parachute?' Ivor radioed back, quiet.

'Not sure. Can't confirm that, yet. It's stuck in a tree like our informants said.'

'Is there a man there, too?' Freddo this time.

'Can't confirm that, either.'

Ivor came wriggling up to join me. 'You're not much cop then, are you? Where is it, butt?'

'By there, look. To the left.'

'Oh yeah.'

'Is it a parachute?' Freddo arrived now, with the others in tow, Aldo flattening ferns and grass as he mowed through the undergrowth like a tank.

Billy wormed his way in beside me. 'There's Reg and his mates. See. Running over by that rock.'

I hadn't noticed them before because they were all ducked down, but now a blob of red bobbed up above the ferns. Reg. He was leading a small group of boys, ducking and weaving, making for the cover of a big grey rock.

The white thing – whatever it was – flapped a bit more in the tree, and Reg and his mates dropped down into the ferns again.

'They're going for it,' said Ivor. 'He's brave, that kid.'

'*Twp*, more like,' said Freddo. 'What if there is a parachutist there, and he's got a gun. They wouldn't stand a chance!'

The sounds of huffing and puffing came drifting up the hill behind us.

PC Richards and Penry Lewis were scrambling up the slope over the rough ground, Ivor's evacuee and his friend egging them on with loud, excited whispers.

'It's not far, mister.'

'He's up here!'

Penry Lewis, out of breath, tried to shush them.

But there wasn't much point, really, because behind this little group was a whole long straggle of noisy people. Old men, in the main, who were part of our Local Defence Volunteers. The Home Guard, people called them. They were supposed to keep us safe if the Germans invaded. Some of them were a bit past it, though, so they were having real trouble getting up the hillside to where we were. Some had old rifles, but one or two waved pitchforks in the air. Dai Owen's grampa had a knife tied onto a broom handle.

Behind this lot trailed a gaggle of girls, Gwenda in charge, chopsing as usual, gas mask in its cardboard box slung over her shoulder with string.

'For goodness' sake, be quiet, will you?' PC Richards stopped in his tracks and half whispered, half shouted at the straggling group.

They were quieter then, though there was still a lot of wheezing and coughing.

When he'd nearly caught up with us, Mr Richards got down on the ground, took off his helmet and slowly crawled up to where we were watching the common. 'What's going on, boys?' He was out of puff, sweating a bit.

'There's a parachutist in that tree, Mr Richards,' Freddo said. 'Over by there!' He pointed to where the white object flapped slowly in the breeze.

'*Duw, duw!*' said Penry Lewis, sliding up beside us. 'There is too!'

'Give us your binoculars, Penry,' PC Richards said.

A little reddish spot bobbed up again in the middle of the green ferns.

'Who on earth is that?' Penry Lewis asked as he struggled to get his binoculars out of their case.

'It's Reg,' Billy said.

'My evacuee,' I said.

'He spotted the parachutist first,' Ivor added.

The little group on the common broke cover again and weaved through the ferns and bushes. We could see them clearly now. Some were carrying sticks.

'Stupid little tyke!' PC Richards muttered, putting the binoculars to his eyes at last.

Freddo shot Ivor a triumphant glance. 'That's what *we* said, Mr Richards.'

'Yes, we did, Mr Richards,' Aldo joined in.

'You're right there, son,' said the policeman. 'That man could be armed.' Then he laughed. With the binoculars still clamped to his eyes, he laughed and laughed. 'That's not a parachute!'

'What is it, Gethin?' asked Penry Lewis.

'It's a newspaper!' he roared. 'Wind must have carried it there.'

He got to his feet and turned to the little group behind him. 'Stand down, boys. It's a newspaper caught in a tree. Danger over.' And he walked forward onto the common.

At that same moment, Reg and the other boys decided to break cover and make a dash for the tree, still some way ahead of them. Because there hadn't been much movement from the 'parachute', they must have reckoned it was safe to go on the attack.

Six or seven bodies went charging through the ferns, moving faster now towards their target, sticks raised, ready. They couldn't see what Mr Richards had seen. They didn't know they were trying to capture an old newspaper.

We ran too, laughing, with Mr Richards and Penry Lewis and one or two of the more active old men.

'It's all right, boys,' Mr Richards shouted across the common, top of his voice. 'It's not a parachute.'

But Reg and the others didn't hear him.

So we joined in, shouting and yelling, leaping over the ferns and the gorse and the bushes like a posse of madmen.

Reg and his mates stopped, taken by surprise, and turned to look at us. Only for a second or two, though, because then we heard him shout out. 'We saw him first. Lay off, will yer? We'll get him. He's ours!'

He urged his boys on, towards the tree.

'He's a twerp, that boy,' Freddo said, happy, laughing.

'Easy mistake, butt,' Ivor came back at him. 'How was he to know?'

We all shouted louder now, when we had breath enough between the laughs, a big burst of voices bouncing over the common.

'Oi, Reg! It's not a parachute.'

'It's a newspaper!'

'You're chasing a newspaper!'

They stopped again. Maybe they'd got the message loud and clear by now. Or maybe they'd got near enough to see what we already knew.

Reg turned to face us as we came racing through the ferns. His cheeks were as red as his hair. His sharp, cunning eyes were narrowed to slits. His friends stood around him, sticks dangling loose in their hands.

We were face to face by now, the two groups.

Us, laughing: not Ivor, though, I noticed.

Them, looking sheepish. Apart from Reg who looked as if he was ready to kill someone.

'Well done, Reginald,' Freddo taunted. 'Is that what you get up to where you come from? Chase old newspapers stuck in trees?'

'Now, now, Frederico,' puffed PC Richards. 'This boy did the right thing.'

'Indeed he did.' Penry Lewis panted up to his side. 'He sent for the authorities. Like everyone's supposed to.'

Gwenda arrived to back up her father. 'Just because it was a false alarm this time doesn't meant that it won't be the real thing next time.'

'Know-all!' Vic whispered, at my side.

Reg's face relaxed, took on some of its old cocky look. 'Only doing my duty, mates,' he said.

'Yes. But it was a newspaper.' Freddo couldn't let it go. 'It was just a newspaper. Any idiot could have seen that if they'd looked properly.' And he laughed again.

Aldo joined in. Me too.

Reg stared at us, smiling, brazen as anything on the surface. But the eyes showed something different. He'd been made to look a fool.

And we'd been there to see it!

Chapter 12

'READ ALL ABOUT IT!'

Freddo was yelling at the top of his voice. 'READ ALL ABOUT IT!'

We swooped up and down the ferny slopes that bordered the path leading home from the common.

'*SOUTH WALES ECHO*! Get your *ECHO* here!' Freddo bawled out, leading the way. He was beside himself with joy at what had happened.

We were laughing too, me and Aldo and Vic and Billy. Ivor wasn't with us. Said he'd go home with Norman, his evacuee. ('Yeah. I bet!' Freddo had whispered to me. 'He's staying behind to suck up to Reg.')

'*SOUTH WALES ECHO!*' Aldo shouted now.

'All the latest news,' Billy chipped in.

'All the headlines,' I added.

Then Freddo shouted, '*EVACUEE MISTAKES OLD NEWSPAPER FOR A DANGEROUS PARACHUTIST.*' He was laughing so much he had to stop running. He doubled over. 'Blummin' heck! I got a stitch.'

The rest of us came to a stop too and flopped down in the ferns.

We were giddy with laughter.

'That was great, that was, aye.' Freddo got his breath back and spread out on the ground with us.

We lay there, on our backs, panting a bit, giggling, squinting up at the sky. The sun was heading west now. Suppertime, nearly.

We'd left the gaggle of people on the common pulling the old paper down from the tree.

'Last Thursday's DAILY EXPRESS,' Penry Lewis had announced.

He'd praised Reg again for sending someone to fetch the police.

'You did your bit,' he'd said.

'So be proud of it,' Gwenda had chipped in, sidling up to Reg.

'Excitement over for today,' Mr Richards had said. 'Time to go home.'

And that's when we'd left, dodging past some of the old men in the Home Guard who were only just arriving on the scene, puffing and blowing, coughing up the coal dust that lay on their lungs from years of working down the pit.

'Coming, Ive?' Freddo had called.

But Ivor had made his excuse about going home with Norman.

Reg was still surrounded by his little group of evacuees, who didn't look quite so sheepish now that they'd got a bit of praise from the grown-ups. Reg himself had stood looking at us, daring us to say more, but we didn't.

Gwenda fluttered round him, flattering him, saying how he might have saved us all from being invaded. Reg smirked. The big hero! The big I AM! Except in our eyes.

'Better get home,' Freddo said now, sitting up in the ferns. We'd stopped laughing, but we knew we'd enjoy remembering this afternoon for a long time to come.

It took us ages to get back to the village, though, because Aldo kept climbing trees and hanging from the branches, free arm flapping, shouting, 'I'm an old newspaper, I am! Come and shoot me down.'

We tried, crawling on our stomachs over the rough and ferny earth, rifles raised, taking aim. But as soon as one of us got near, Aldo would drop down in a shower of twigs and leaves and crush his victim to bits.

Then the game would start all over again as, tree by tree, we made our slow way home.

When we got to the edge of the village, we said, 'Ta-ra. See you tomorrow!' to Vic and Billy, and made our way down Cardiff Road to Moretti's café.

PC Richards waved to us from the window of the police station as we passed. 'Where've you boys been till now?' he mouthed through the glass.

'Playing,' we mouthed back.

'Your suppertime soon,' he said. 'Go on home!'

'Oh, no! Is it that late?' Freddo said. 'Mamma'll give us a right telling-off.'

So we ran the last few hundred yards to the shop corner. Mrs Moretti was standing in the doorway, face like thunder.

'Told you,' Freddo panted to his brother.

But as we got nearer, we could all see that really she looked more frightened than angry. Her face was ash white, her eyes brimming with tears. She waved the boys closer. 'Quick! Quick!'

'What's the matter, Mamma? What's happened?' Aldo, worried, ran to meet her. Freddo and me came to a stop a few steps away.

Mrs Moretti spoke to the boys, urgently, in Italian, and tried to hurry Aldo in through the open shop door.

'What is it, Fred?' I asked, hoping he would translate what was going on. I thought that something must have happened to Mr Moretti, an accident or something.

'Go home, Robert.' She spoke to me now, in English, her voice sharp, frightened. 'Your nanna will be waiting for you.'

Freddo stepped up to the doorway. He spoke in Italian too. He never did that when I was around. Never.

'What is it, Fred?' I asked. 'Is your dad all right?'

'He's all right, Robert.' Mrs Moretti succeeded in getting Aldo into the shop and pulled at Freddo's shirt sleeve to get him in too. 'The boys will see you later. All right?'

'Yes. A'right. But what's going on?'

'Italy's come into the war,' Freddo whispered.

'Inside, Frederico!' His mother spoke sharply, yanked at his arm.

'On Hitler's side,' Freddo added.

'Inside, Frederico. Now!' Mrs Moretti took a firmer grip of his arm and started pulling him towards the door.

Then more words in Italian, but she was whispering too, almost as if she didn't want anyone else to hear.

Mr Moretti came to the doorway. 'Lena. Shush! Stop fussing. There are people in the shop.'

'I'm not fussing. I just want these boys in the house.'

'When did it happen, Dad?' Freddo asked. 'How did you find out?'

'It was on the wireless, Frederico. On the news.'

Aldo had pushed his way back out onto the doorstep. 'What's going to happen, Papa?'

'Nothing, Aldo. Don't you worry,' his father said. 'Everything's going to be all right.'

'It will be, Papa, won't it?' Aldo looked at his father, begging. 'Because we're Welsh. We're Welsh, aren't we, Mamma?'

But Mrs Moretti didn't say anything. She pursed her lips and pushed her way through the three of them, back into the shop.

'Yes. You're Welsh,' said Mr Moretti, taking hold of Aldo's hand, patting it. 'You were born here. You'll be all right.'

Freddo looked at his dad. Eye to eye.

Neither of them said anything.

Aldo stared at them, wondering at the silence, not understanding what they both knew.

That Mr Moretti hadn't been born here.

That he was Italian.

That he was the enemy now.

Chapter 13

'Better get inside, boys.' Mr Moretti cleared his throat and turned back into the shop.

'Wait till the news gets out and things have a chance to calm down. Tell young Robert you'll see him later.'

So Aldo said, 'See you later, Bob.'

'Right, Al. See you later.'

'See you, Bob,' said Freddo.

'See you, Fred.'

They followed their dad into the café.

I set off down the street to have my dinner with Nanna, and Reg if he was back. Now, I was a secret agent, dodging from doorway to doorway, keeping my eye on my suspect (Mrs Pritchard's cat, which was slinking down the road ahead of me).

But I didn't feel much like playing, really. Not any more. There was too much to think about. I knew that in Cardiff some Germans had been rounded up and taken to a sort of detention camp, even though they'd been living here for years. I wondered if the same thing was going to happen to the Italians.

Nanna didn't do much to stop me worrying. She'd heard the news on her wireless, of course. She sat in her chair, by the big wooden sideboard, dabbing at her eyes.

'Poor Lena! Poor Pete.' Mr Moretti's real name was Pietro but my family always called him Pete.

'Heat the stew up, will you, love?' Nanna went on. 'I'm feeling a bit peckish.'

I moved over to the stove and struck a match to light the biggest gas ring. 'What'll happen to them, Nanna?' I asked, knowing she wouldn't know really, but wanting her to say it was all going to be all right.

'I don't know, boy. But there's always trouble for someone, isn't there?' She dabbed at her eyes again.

I lifted the pan of stew onto the hissing gas.

The front door slammed and Reg came into the kitchen. He went and stood by Nanna's chair. Breezy as ever, he was. 'Hello, Nan. How're you doing?'

'Oh, a bit sad today, boy.'

'Why's that then, Nan?'

I stirred the stew, not looking at him, not wanting to hear him buttering up my nanna – and her falling for it.

She dabbed at her eyes again. 'That Mussolini have come into the war on Hitler's side.'

'Oh dear. Do you think that'll mean trouble for your Italian friends, Nan?'

'That's what I'm worried about, Reginald.'

'Yeah, I can see you would be. What a shame, eh?'

I went on stirring the stew, swede and fatty meat mostly, waiting for him to get tired of smarming up to Nanna and turn his attention to me.

He did. 'Hello, Robert.' He moved round the table to where I was standing. 'Where've you been today?'

'Up the common,' I said.

Then, quick as anything, he came up close behind me and twisted my free arm behind my back. He was bigger than me and stronger and I winced with the pain.

'Up the common, eh?' He tightened his hold on my arm and twisted it further. 'Anything exciting happen on the common, this afternoon, then?' His grip tightened again.

I caught my breath, let the spoon drop in the stew, and tried to twist away from him. But he was strong, all right, and he was still angry because we'd laughed at him. This was part of his revenge, and he knew he could get away with it because he also knew that Nanna couldn't see what was going on.

Unless I shouted out and told her. And I wasn't going to do that. Not yet, anyway.

'Answer the boy, Robert.' Nanna looked in our direction, unseeing. 'Don't be rude.'

'Nothing!' I grunted.

'Nothing?' he mimicked. 'Must have been boring, eh, Nan?'

The pain was really bad now. I bent down, trying to free myself from his grip, but he twisted his body too, so that he could keep a hold on me.

Nanna said, 'You must have been doing something, Robert. Who were you with?'

'Freddo and Aldo and the others,' I gasped.

'What on earth's the matter with you, Robert?' Nanna said, sharp. 'Got a frog in your throat?' She was getting suspicious now.

With a final, vicious twist, Reg brought me to the floor and chirped, 'Stew's boiling over!'

I lay on the floor, nursing my arm, tears springing to my eyes. But I wiped them away quickly. I wasn't going to give him the satisfaction of seeing he'd made me cry.

'For heaven's sake, Robert. What you doing?' Nanna made to get up from her chair and feel her way to the stove. 'You're supposed to be minding the stew!'

'Don't you worry yourself, Nan,' said Reg and gave me a little farewell kick as he moved across the kitchen to sit her down again. 'Everything's under control. I'm here to look after you.'

'Aw,' she said, settling back into her chair. 'There's a lovely boy you are.'

I got to my feet, sniffling a bit. My arm was aching. My pride was wounded worse though. I turned off the gas under the saucepan. Sticking out of the bubbling, fatty stew was the handle of the spoon that I'd dropped in it. With my fingers, I fished it out, very carefully, and dried it on the dishcloth.

Reg smirked at me across the room.

'Are you coming to the table, Nanna?' I asked, spooning the lumps of meat and vegetables into chipped white bowls.

'Yes.' She eased herself up again, Reg leaping to her side, helping her to a chair.

My face was burning, but not from the heat of the stove. I sniffed again to hold back another spring of tears.

'Why are you sniffing, Robert? What's wrong with you today?' Nanna settled herself at the table, her hands fumbling around for a spoon.

'Got a cold coming, Nanna. That's all.' I sniffed down the last of the tears and put her bowl of stew down in front of her. I guided her hand to the edge of the bowl.

'In June?' Reg scoffed.

'A summer cold, Reginald,' Nanna said, starting to eat. 'They can be bad!'

'You wanna watch that, then, butt!' said Reg. 'Might stop you going to play with your mates on the common.' He came over to the stove and spooned out a bowlful of stew for himself.

I stood back and let him do it, then filled a bowl for myself.

Outside, in the street, there was some shouting. Feet pounded the pavement.

'What's that?' Nanna stopped eating, turned her head towards the front door, listening.

'Dunno, Nan,' said Reg. 'D'you want me to go and have a look?'

He went through into the front passage.

'Maybe someone's spotted a parachutist!' I called after him, but I sat down and drew my chair close to Nanna as I said it. I don't think he heard me, though, because the commotion was growing. More people running, shouting.

'Up the café,' someone called out. 'Moretti's!'

I stood up, heart pounding. Nanna, spoon halfway towards her mouth, stew dribbling back into the bowl, listened even more intently.

Then, my mother's voice at the door. 'Oh God. It's terrible,' she said, coming wild-eyed into the kitchen, her brown factory apron flapping round her as she walked through the door.

Reg followed, asking what the matter was.

'It's awful!' she wailed, scaring me now, for I had never seen or heard my mother in such a state.

'What is it, Myra?' Nanna was worried too even though she couldn't see my mother's face. 'What's happened?'

My mother flopped into a chair, crying. 'They're attacking Moretti's café,' she said.

Chapter 14

'Dear God!' Nanna half rose from her chair. 'The Germans, is it? Have they landed?'

'No, Mam,' my mother said. 'It's not the Germans. It's people from round here.'

'What for?' I asked, but I already knew the answer.

So did Reg. 'They're our enemies now, ain't they, the Eye . . . the Italians? Now that Mussoloony's come into the war on Adolf's side?'

My mother rounded on him, sharp, angry. 'The Morettis aren't our enemies! They've been living here for years. They're our friends.' She sat down at the table.

'Yeah, you're right of course, Mrs Prosser,' Reg wheedled his way back into her good books, and sat down next to her. 'But you know what people are like. Tarring everyone with the same brush . . . and that . . .' He tailed away, lost for words because the words he wanted to say, really, weren't going to go down too well with us.

'Who's doing it, Myra?' Nanna asked, sitting again now, chewing hard on a piece of fatty meat.

'Oh, the usual bunch of hotheads,' Mam said. She reached into the pocket of her apron, took out a packet of cigarettes and a box of matches. 'Terry Williams it is, and that bunch from Edwards Street.'

Nanna tutted, 'Aye. Aye. Might have known they'd be mixed up in it.'

'What they been doing, Mam?' I asked, scared.

'Smashing up the shop.' She lit her cigarette and reached out to the sideboard for the green glass ashtray. 'Ten jars of sweets broken already and some tables and chairs.'

'How do you know, My? Who told you?' Nanna asked.

'I met Betty Howells on the way home,' my mam said. 'She was in there when Williams came in and started throwing his weight around.'

She blew out a big puff of smoke. 'Make me some tea, Robert, will you?'

'Yes.' I filled the kettle at the bosh and lit the gas stove.

Mam went on, telling us what she'd heard, '"This shop belongs to us now," shouts Terry Williams. "You can clear out, you Eyeties!" That's what Betty said.'

'Drunk!' said Nanna, in disgust.

'Where's Freddo and Aldo?' I put the kettle on the gas and turned back to my mam.

Reg was leaning on the table, looking straight at her, putting on a sympathetic face.

'I don't know, Robert,' she said, a bit sadly.

'I'm going to see if they're all right,' I said.

'No, you're not! You keep away.' She took another puff of her cigarette. 'There's enough people up there already. It's going to get worse before it gets better.'

'I won't get involved, Mam. I promise.' I didn't know how I could help Fred and Al if they were in trouble, but I wanted to be there just in case there *was* anything I could do.

'No, Robert! I've said, haven't I?'

'Oh please, Mam. They're my butties.'

'NO!' she shouted, stubbing out her cigarette, getting angry. 'There's probably a hundred people up there by now. God knows what could happen.'

'I'll go with him, Mrs Prosser,' Reg chipped in. 'I'll keep an eye on him.'

'There you are, Myra,' Nanna said. 'Reginald's a strong lad. He'll keep the boy safe.'

'NO!' It was my turn to shout now. 'I don't want *him* to come with me.'

'It's the only way you're going,' said my mother, softening up a bit. 'If I let either of you go, that is.'

'It'll be curfew time soon,' I protested. 'He can't be out after curfew.' (The evacuees were all supposed to be indoors before nine o'clock.)

'Don't let that worry you, Rob,' said Reg, making out like he was my best friend. 'I'll say I'm on an errand for your ma. It's worked before.'

He gave Mam a big wink.

She gave a little laugh, calming down now from her fright and worry. 'You're a cheeky little blighter, in't you?' she said, brushing some stray ash off the table, smiling though.

'You're right there, My,' Nanna joined in, spooning up the last mouthful of soup. 'He's not backward in coming forward, is he?'

'Gets me places,' he laughed.

103

'I can go on my own!' I jumped up, spoiling their little party.

'No, you can't,' said my mother, sharp again. 'The only way you're going is if Reg goes with you. And you're back in ten minutes. Right?'

I knew I wasn't going to win this one. I'd have to go with him. Well, leave the house with him anyway. Then we could go our separate ways. I knew he'd want to be rid of me as much as I was keen to get shot of him.

'A'right, then,' I muttered.

'Stay out of trouble,' my mother warned. 'And back here when I say. Don't forget.'

'Righty'o!' said Reg, pushing back his chair, getting up from the table, giving her a big smile. 'And don't you worry. I'll have your little Robert back safe and sound in ten minutes.'

Another smile and a wink. 'Or thereabouts.'

Then we were both out of the door before my mother could change her mind. We heard her, shouting after us: 'Ten minutes, mind!'

Chapter 15

We legged it along the street, taking separate pavements. People were out on their doorsteps, looking up towards the corner where a big crowd of people had gathered outside Moretti's café.

'What's going on, Robert?' Mrs Pritchard stood at her door, stroking her fat cat.

'Don't know!' I yelled back as I raced past.

'Come and tell me when you come back, will you, there's a good boy?'

'A'right,' I lied.

I don't know how many people were outside Moretti's. There might have been a hundred, like Mam said, or there might have been more. Mostly it was young men, like Terry Williams and his cronies. But there were older people, too, and some kids.

The shop was locked, full of shadows. No sign of Freddo and Al or their mam and dad.

Some young men in the crowd were shouting a bit, mostly rubbish as far as I could tell. 'Give us what you've got, Moretti!'

'This shop belongs to us now!'

They jostled and yelled and pushed each other forward towards the big glass window. A couple raised their fists. Some girls cheered them on. There was a lot of swearing. Someone spat, and the big gob of spit trickled down the pane.

PC Richards pushed through the crowd, trying to get at the ringleaders. Red-faced and sweating, he tried to calm things down, but the noise and the excitement had stirred people up, and he couldn't get very far. 'Come on now, boys!' he puffed. 'You've had your fun. Time to call it a day!'

A hand reached out of the crowd behind him, slipped off his chinstrap and threw his helmet high into the air. A few people cheered.

'That's enough of that!' he blustered. 'You're all heading for a whole lot of trouble!' He pushed his way back out of the crowd, scrabbling for his helmet.

'Why don't you arrest them, Gethin?' a woman called out. 'It's a disgrace what's going on here.'

'Don't be daft, Vera!' he snapped back. 'There's only me. I've phoned Pontfechan to send help. Then there'll be some arrests, don't you worry.'

Off he went down the street, mopping his forehead with a big white hankie, to wait for reinforcements.

The shouting and pushing was getting louder now, nastier. 'Show your face, Moretti.'

'Come on out, you spies!'

The men at the front of the crowd started chanting. 'SPIES! SPIES! SPIES!' The sound echoed down the street, loud, ugly. 'SPIES! SPIES! SPIES!'

Where Reg had got to in all this, I didn't know. Then I saw a familiar red head bobbing up on the far side of the crowd. He was talking to someone whose face I couldn't see because of the crush of people. His eyes were shining; he was chopsing away like mad, caught up in the mood of the thing.

The crowd parted and I saw who he was with. Ivor, just as excited, was gazing at the shopfront, craning his neck, talking to Reg like they'd been best friends for ever.

Then Ivor saw me, said something to Reg, and they both laughed.

I didn't care, because all I was really concerned about was where the Morettis were. 'Are they still in the house?' I shouted above the screaming and swearing.

Mrs Rees, our teacher's wife, was standing next to me. 'I think so, Robert,' she said. 'Nobody's seen them leave, anyway.' She stood on tiptoe to see over the people in front of her. 'Does your mam know you're here?'

'Yes,' I said, and thought that our ten minutes must nearly be up by now and we should be getting home. But I couldn't go, not yet. I needed to know where Fred and Aldo were.

Someone at the front shouted, 'There he is, look. The swine's in the shop.' There was a big roar and everyone pushed forward, heads craning to see.

Inside the café, a figure was moving towards the shop door. Mr Moretti.

'Come on out!' Terry Williams, the ringleader, yelled. 'Let's see how brave you are.'

'Shame on you!' a woman cried, but not at Mr Moretti. At Williams and the little group of men who were doing most of the shouting. 'He haven't done you no harm.'

'He's an Eyetie, in'e?' they yelled back.

'They're our enemies now,' one of them said.

'Enemy aliens,' yelled another. 'Should be interned, they should.'

'Put them away!' someone else shouted. 'Send them to prison.'

Mrs Rees leaned forward to scold the group of young men at the front of the crowd. 'That's enough of that,' she shouted. 'There's children in there.'

'What? That big lad. He isn't a kid any more.' It was Terry Williams again, the one who had started it. His friends laughed, then one of them pointed into the shop and said, 'Oi, look! He's going!'

The shadowy shape inside the café had turned away. Maybe Mr Moretti had come into the shop to put up the blackout curtains. Or maybe he'd even thought of coming out to reason with the crowd, but then he'd seen how ugly things were and had moved back, into the kitchen behind the counter.

'COWARD!' Terry Williams yelled, and suddenly there was a great crash. The big shop window cracked and splintered. Someone had put a brick through the glass.

People screamed and shouted even louder and the men at the front pushed forward. Across the heads of the crowd, Reg jumped up and down, beside himself with excitement. I was excited too, I have to say, what with all the noise. Mostly though, I was scared. What would happen to my friends now?

Terry Williams lumbered forward, pushing against the broken glass, trying to force his way into the shop. 'Come on, boys. Let's go and help ourselves.'

'You're thieves, you are,' a man shouted.

'Call yourselves patriots,' yelled someone else. 'You're just thieves.'

'Stop them, then,' said Mrs Rees, next to me, turning around to look for support.

But no one dared. The bullies were winning again, it looked like.

There was a movement in one of the windows upstairs. You could hardly see it unless you were looking for it. A face peeped out from behind the net curtain. A pale, frightened face.

Aldo!

Had anyone else seen him? I didn't think so. They were all busy watching the last, pointed spikes of glass being kicked out of the downstairs window.

'Al!' I wanted to call out. 'Get away from the window before they see you! Get away!' I couldn't, though, because that would only have drawn attention to him.

He stood there, staring, wide-eyed, gazing down at the hate below.

The first few young men were stepping through into the shop now, laughing, eager to fill their pockets with money and chocolate and cigarettes.

I didn't know what to do, didn't know how I could protect my friends. I couldn't, really. Couldn't do anything. I knew that. I just had to stand and watch as the mob pushed into the shop.

The noise got louder: shouts and yells and some booing now, against the thieves.

There was another movement behind the curtain at the upstairs window. Another face came to stare down at the crowd. Freddo this time, as pale and as scared as his brother.

I looked across at where Reg and Ivor were standing. Something told me they'd have seen the boys too.

I was right. The pair of them were staring up at the bedroom window, faces shining with excitement – and nastiness. Reg began to raise his arm, finger ready to point, mouth opening to call out, to alert the crowd to the hiding boys.

'No!' I pushed my way through the mass of people, elbowing, ducking, sidling. I wanted to stop him giving the game away, but the press of people was too great. I pushed, harder and harder, but I couldn't make headway fast enough.

Then whistles blew. 'It's the Pontfechan police!' someone shouted.

'And about time too!' said someone else.

Up the street ran ten or twelve policemen, truncheons raised, PC Richards urging them on.

One of the young men, straddled in the window frame between shop and pavement, raised the alarm. 'Boys! It's the bobbies! Get out! Quick!'

They tumbled through the window then, hands full of cigarette packets, sweets, chocolate bars, dropping some in their hurry to get through the crowd and away from the police. A couple of kids bent down and scooped up the chocolates, stuffed them in their pockets and scurried off too.

PC Richards came puffing through the crowd. 'Out of the way! Out of the way!' Whistles blew. People scattered.

The faces at the upstairs window disappeared.

A hand gripped me round the neck. 'Ten minutes, I

said!' My mam. 'Where's Reg?' She turned me round, but held on tight to my shirt collar.

'Here I am, Mrs Prosser.' He came hurrying through the crowds, which were thinning out now the police had arrived. 'I was just coming to get Robert. Didn't want to leave his friends, though. Couldn't get him to come home.'

'Liar!' I screamed. 'You liar.'

I kicked out at him but he did a neat side-swerve and I ended up kicking Mrs Rees on the ankle.

'Ouch!' she yelped. 'Be careful, Robert!'

My mother apologised for me. 'Sorry, Mrs Rees.' Then her grip tightened round my neck again. 'Home!' she barked. 'The pair of you.'

She gave me a shove that sent me flying halfway down the street. Well, that's what it felt like, anyway.

Reg followed behind, chatting, telling her the full story, but careful to make it sound as if he was on the Morettis' side.

The men who'd broken into the shop had scattered, police chasing them, whistles still blowing.

As I looked back up the street, I thought I saw the same two pale faces at the upstairs window.

Freddo and Aldo, my friends.

Enemy aliens!

And scared for their lives.

Chapter 16

'Now,' said Mr Rees, standing in front of the blackboard, his eyes taking in the whole of the class. '*I* know that all of *you* know what happened last night at Moretti's café.'

'Yes, Mr Rees,' thirty voices piped up.

'I *also* know that some of you were there. In person.' The eyes focussed in on me. 'Am I right, Robert Prosser?'

'Yes, Mr Rees.'

Faces turned to look at where I was sitting, among them Billy's and Vic's.

'Were you?' Vic mouthed, wide-eyed.

Ivor turned round too, of course, unblinking. Seems like *he* hadn't been spotted in the crowd because Mr Rees went on, 'Because of what took place – and I'm sure Robert will be able to give you a full description at playtime – Frederico won't be with us this morning.'

I already knew that. On my way to school, I'd passed the café. Someone had been there to nail boards across the broken window.

Mr Moretti was out on the pavement, sweeping away the last of the glass. 'Hello, Roberto. Off to school, then?'

'Yes. Is Freddo ready?'

'He won't be going this morning. Maybe tomorrow . . . see how things are. Yes?' He swept the last splinters of glass into the gutter.

'Is Aldo staying in too?' I asked.

'Yes. Just until things calm down a bit.' He still thought 'things' would calm down. I was scared they wouldn't.

I was still worrying about it when Mr Rees said, 'Let's forget about last night for now, and get on with our work. Get your spelling books out.'

We opened our desks and took out the battered exercise books where we made our spelling lists.

'Mr Rees?' Philip Humphreys put his hand up.

'Yes, Philip?'

'How do you spell "alien"?'

People laughed, including Ivor, I saw.

'Why do want to know that, boy? It's not on our spelling list, is it?'

'No, Mr Rees. But I heard someone saying Freddo was an alien.' More laughter. '. . . and I'd never heard it before.'

'Where've you been living?' Trevor Davies muttered. 'Never heard of enemy aliens.'

'*You* obviously have, Trevor Davies,' said Mr Rees. 'Would you care to explain what the term means?'

'It's like Germans who live here are enemy aliens,' said Trevor. 'Because they're not British citizens . . . and because we're at war with Germany . . . that makes them enemy aliens.'

'Like the Italians,' Evan Griffiths said.

'Like the Morettis,' Colin Vickers said.

'Like Freddo and Aldo,' Ivor said. 'They are now, aren't they, Mr Rees?'

'Well, technically speaking, I suppose they are . . .'

Mr Rees said, looking uncomfortable, '. . . but let's wait and see what happens, shall we, before we start calling people names?'

Ivor turned in his chair to face me, smiling, crafty. 'Are you still going to be Freddo's friend then, Bob?'

'Yes. Suppose so. Why not?'

Ivor turned back again to face the teacher. 'He'll be talking to the enemy then, won't he, Mr Rees?'

'Conspiring!' said Trevor.

'Now, now, that's enough.' Mr Rees wanted to bring this to a close. 'I'm sure Robert and Frederico will be able to stay friends.' He turned to write on the blackboard. 'Copy these ten words into your books.'

Business finished, he thought. Except it wasn't, of course.

At morning playtime, Vic and Billy and I were playing boxing kangaroos. Billy had seen them in the theatre in Cardiff when his auntie had taken him once for a treat. Billy was the kangaroo, me and Vic were the boxers, trying to land a punch as he bounced around.

'Tommy Farr, I am,' said Vic, puffing. He was a famous boxer, Welsh.

Billy had asked Ivor if he wanted to join in, but he said it was a daft game, and anyway, he wasn't sure that he wanted to play with someone who was palling up with the enemy.

'*Twpsyn*!' Vic had muttered under his breath, as he walked off, and we got on with our playing.

Then we saw Ivor and some of the other boys run over to the fence that separated our part of the playground from the seniors. The older boys had called them over. The group grew and so did the chatter.

Billy stopped bouncing. So did I. Vic went on ducking and weaving for a bit, then he stopped too when he saw some of the boys break away from the fence and come towards us.

'Oi, butt!' shouted Ivor, leading the group. 'Listen to this.' He came closer, pleased with himself about something.

'They're going to round up all the Eyeties. Mr Churchill said.'

Mr Churchill was the Prime Minister.

'How'd you know?' Billy asked.

'The seniors just told us,' Ivor gloated. 'They been listening to the wireless. He's going to round them up and put them in camps.'

'Internment camps,' said Evan Griffiths.

'Collar the lot!' announced Trevor, pushing forward. 'That's what Churchill said he'd do. Collar the lot!'

The words rippled round the group, satisfying to say. 'Collar the lot . . . Collar the lot.'

'Everyone?' asked Vic.

'All the Italians?' That was me asking, though I wasn't sure I wanted to hear the answer.

'Not all,' said Trevor.

'Not yet,' said Ivor. Then, turning to the boys nearest him, he whispered, just loud enough, 'More's the pity.'

A few of them laughed at that, and he went on, 'All the men over sixteen, if they haven't been living here for . . . how many years, Trev?'

'Twenty,' said Trevor. 'If they haven't been living here for twenty years.'

Ivor came up close, almost eyeball to eyeball. 'How long's old Moretti been here, Bob?'

'Dunno,' I said. 'A long time.'

'Yeah, but how long, Bob?' Billy asked.

'A long time. I told you!'

Then someone said, 'How old is Aldo?'

'If he's over sixteen,' said someone else, 'he'll get rounded up, won't he?'

'He's fifteen,' I said, defiantly, but to tell the truth, I wasn't sure.

Asking Aldo his real age had never seemed to matter.

Until now.

Chapter 17

'How old do you think Aldo is, Nanna?'

School was over for the day. We were having our dinner, potatoes and gravy, just me and her at the kitchen table.

She'd heard the news on the wireless about rounding up the Italian men, so she knew why I was asking. 'Don't you worry, boy. He'll be all right.'

'I know that, Nanna.' I mashed up the potatoes on my plate into the thick brown gravy and forked it into my mouth. 'But do you know how old he is? Really?'

Nanna tried to spear one of her potatoes but it went skidding across the table top.

'Shall I mash your potatoes up, Nanna?' I asked, skewering the potato back onto her plate.

'Why not,' she nodded. 'And give me a spoon to eat with, love . . . but don't tell your mam.'

'A'right. But how old is he, do you think?'

She waited for me to mash up her dinner. 'Well, the Morettis came to Tregwyn when Aldo was a tiny baby . . .'

'When was that, then? What year?'

'Give me a chance, Robert, there's a good boy. I'm havin' a think.'

I took out a spoon from the table drawer and put it in her hand.

'It was the same year that your mam and dad got married.' Nanna took the spoon and felt for her plate. 'I know that because we had an ice-cream cake to celebrate . . . and the Morettis were new in the village then. Hadn't long come from Italy.' She sucked potatoes off her spoon. 'Very posh, that was, to have an ice-cream cake!'

'So what year was it, Nanna?'

'1925,' she said, licking her lips.

'That makes Aldo fifteen then, don' it?' I felt relieved, comforted.

'Coming up sixteen,' said Nanna, spooning up another mouthful, 'depending on which month his birthday is.'

I couldn't stand any more of this. I needed to know for definite. I needed to see my friends, to find out what was happening.

I got up from my place and forked up the last mouthfuls of my dinner. I carried my plate to the bosh and put it in the tin washing-up bowl.

'I've finished my dinner, Nanna. I'm going out.'

'Where to?'

'Out, that's all.' I couldn't tell her I was going to the Morettis because I thought she would try to stop me.

'You be careful then.'

'Course I will.' I turned on the tap and let the cold water rinse the gravy off the plate.

'You've got to watch out, these days,' Nanna went on. 'Someone reported a parachutist on the common yesterday.'

'Who told you that, Nanna?' The last of the gravy washed away down the plughole.

'Reginald did,' said Nanna. 'He tells me things, that boy.' She slipped another spoonful of food into her mouth, her eyes seeking me out. 'Like *you* used to,' she sighed.

I turned off the tap and left the plate in the bowl.

'Good thing Reg was there,' Nanna went on. 'He got up close enough to see what it really was. An old newspaper . . .' And she chuckled with pleasure at brave Reg's discovery.

'So Reg found that out, did he?'

'Yes. Lucky someone was on the alert.'

'Yes. Lucky,' I said and wiped my hands on my trousers. I didn't want to know any more about how the ace spy had saved the day. 'I'm off now,' I said and made for the passage.

'Put the wireless on for me before you go then.' There was some cheery music on which seemed to please Nanna, so I got out of the house without any more conversation.

In the afternoon sun, there were only a few people around. Just a couple of women talking their way up the street, on their way to see if there was anything to buy in the shops, and Mr Yoxall, on his way home from morning shift at the pit, his face black with coal dust. There were pit baths but some men would rather come home and wash.

'Hello, Robert,' he said. 'Any news from your dad?'

'No, Mr Yoxall,' I said, scooting past. 'Not yet!'

'Oh well, no news is good news. Tell your mam I was asking.'

'I will, Mr Yoxall,' I said, running on.

Moretti's café was still boarded up where the men had broken through into the shop, but there was a little note pinned on it now.

BUSINESS AS USUAL, it said.

Through the open door, I could see Mr Moretti behind the counter, his back to me, wiping down the shelves where the sweet bottles usually stood. The shelves were almost empty now and in the spaces between the few jars that were left, someone had put some fancy ice-cream bowls and glasses to fill up the gaps.

There were no customers.

Mr Moretti turned and saw me hanging around in the doorway.

'Come in, Roberto,' he said, wiping his hands on the cloth he'd been using. 'We're open.'

In I went. 'I haven't come to buy anything, Mr Moretti.'

'That's all right. There's not a lot left to buy.' He lifted the little hatch in the counter and stepped out to meet me. His face was smiling, but I thought he seemed very sad.

'Come to see the boys, then, have you?'

'Yes.'

'They're in the kitchen. Go through.'

I hesitated. Why? Was I scared that someone in the street would see me?

'Don't be such a *twpsyn!*' I told myself, and walked

through the empty shop to the door that led into the kitchen at the back.

There were fewer chairs and tables than usual in the café, so some of them must have got smashed up when the men broke in last night.

Mr Moretti called out, 'Lena. Boys. There's someone to see you!'

The kitchen door sprang open as I reached for the handle. Mrs Moretti stood in the doorway. It was like she'd been there, waiting behind the door. 'Oh, Robert. It's only you!' Her voice shook.

In Italian, she let fly at Mr Moretti. I couldn't understand the words, but I could understand the meaning. She was angry with him at not saying who the 'someone to see you' was. She was frightened; that was clear to me too. Her face was white, her eyes red. Instead of the neat way she tied her hair back, today it hung loose around her face.

'Young Roberto has come to see his friends, Lena.' Mr Moretti came up close behind me, patient, smiling. 'Let him in.'

'Yes.' She was flustered, apologetic. 'Come through, Robert.'

I'd only been in the Morettis' kitchen a couple of times before. It wasn't bare and dull, like ours. There was lots of furniture packed in here: comfy chairs and a couch and a big table underneath the window that looked out on the yard.

Before, when I'd been, there were boxes piled under the stairs that went up to the bedrooms. Boxes of sweets and chocolates and cigarettes ready to be taken

121

through to the shop when the shelves got empty. Not today, though.

The other big difference to our house was that the Morettis had lots of pictures on their walls. Sunny skies and blue seas, mostly, but there was a big religious picture too, of a woman holding a baby, with angels floating around her head. Strings of black beads were hung round the picture frame, and a little wooden cross was tucked in the top where it sat against the wall.

'Bob!' Aldo struggled up from one of the comfy chairs and came to give me a hug. I couldn't dodge this one because his mother was looking. 'You came to see us.'

'Hiya, Bob.' Freddo looked up from his book and winked as Aldo released me, panting, from his grip. Freddo looked as red-eyed and tired as his mam.

There was a man in the room who I hadn't seen before. A chubby man, with twinkling eyes, but with a face that certainly wasn't laughing.

'Aren't you going to introduce us, Frederico?' he asked from the chair by the big black stove where he was sitting.

'This is Uncle Gino,' said Freddo. 'From over Deri.'

'Hello,' I said.

'Hello . . . Robert?' said Uncle Gino. 'Very nice to meet any loyal friend of my lovely nephews.'

He turned back to talk to Mrs Moretti who'd closed the kitchen door and was at the stove now, boiling a pan of water with something white and stringy in it.

'He's the one Gwenda was talking about,' Freddo whispered as he waved me over to join him on the sofa. 'The one they found with a gun.'

122

I looked at Uncle Gino with a new respect, and sat down next to Freddo. I peered, sideways, at his book. It was the latest Biggles story, *Biggles Goes to War*.

Aldo crashed down onto the couch with us.

'Oof! Be careful, Al!' Freddo pleaded, as the two of us were crammed together, elbow banging elbow.

'Sorry, Fred,' said Aldo. 'Didn't mean to hurt you.'

'I know that, Al. Just be careful, will you? Don't know your own strength, mun.'

'We saw you last night, Bob,' Aldo offered.

'Oh.'

I didn't know what else to say.

'Shush, Al,' Freddo hissed. 'Mamma doesn't want us to talk about it.'

'Fair dos,' said Aldo.

We went on looking at the book for a bit, not really reading, but I didn't like to ask the question I'd come to ask – how old Aldo really was – while the grown-ups were in the room.

Mrs Moretti and Uncle Gino were jabbering away in Italian, their conversation getting more and more heated. He seemed to be angry with her for some reason.

Freddo looked up from his book, listening to what they were saying.

His mam was getting upset, I could see. 'What's the matter, Fred?' I asked, quietly.

'Nothing,' he lied. 'Family thing.'

Aldo, ever helpful, whispered in my ear, 'He's saying there's nothing to worry about because we've been living here a long time. Mamma doesn't believe him.'

'Shut up, Al!' his brother hissed at him, across me.

'Right-o!'

Freddo threw down his book. 'We're going outside,' he announced.

His mother broke off her argument with Uncle Gino. 'Where outside?'

'Outside, in the yard, that's all.'

'Oh. Go on then.' She spoke to the boys in Italian again, warning them, I guess, to take care, even in the backyard.

The three of us trooped through the outhouse, full of shining metal vats where Mr Moretti used to make his ice cream, and down the steps into the yard at the back of the café.

'Do you think your uncle's right, Fred? Do you think anything will happen to your dad?' I had to ask, but I was scared of what the answer would be.

The two of us perched on the steps. Aldo picked up a ball and started heading it against the high back wall. Someone had chalked a goalpost on it.

'When my mam and dad came from Italy,' said Freddo, 'they could have taken an oath to be loyal to the British king. But they didn't get round to it. Uncle Gino did. That's why he's angry with them.'

'So, if your dad had taken this oath, he might not get . . .' I didn't know how to finish my sentence. Taken away? Rounded up? Interned? None of them sounded very nice.

But I didn't have to finish the sentence off anyway, because Freddo said, 'I don't know. None of us knows what's going to happen.'

He was talking quietly, didn't want Aldo to hear, didn't want him to be upset.

We looked at him, happily leading his team to victory as he landed ball after ball in the net.

I paused. Then, 'Freddo,' I asked, 'how old is Al?'

The answer came back sharp, ready. 'He's fifteen, Bob. He's not sixteen for another six months. In December!'

'That's good,' I said, as Aldo scored another goal.

Chapter 18

'I'm off now, boys.' Uncle Gino came to the door at the top of the yard steps.

'Ta-ta then, Uncle Gino,' said Aldo, picking up the ball as it bounced back from the goal.

'You be good strong boys, eh? Do what your mamma and papa tell you.'

'We will, Uncle Gino,' said Freddo, climbing the steps to kiss his uncle on the cheek.

'That's my Frederico!' said his uncle, smiling now to match his twinkling eyes. He kissed Freddo on the cheek too.

'No kiss from you, Aldo?' he said.

Aldo bounded across the yard and up the steps. Freddo and me dodged aside to let him through. Aldo gave his uncle a big hug and kissed him on the cheek too.

Uncle Gino pulled a face because he was getting a bit crushed, but his smile warmed into a laugh. He wriggled free of Aldo and stretched out his hand to shake mine. 'It was nice to meet you, Robert. Thank you for coming to see the boys.'

'That's all right,' I mumbled back, embarrassed, stepping up to take his hand. I didn't know any grown-ups who shook hands with kids, or let themselves be kissed on the cheek by their nephews.

Mrs Moretti called from the kitchen, 'Time to eat.'

Uncle Gino gave the boys one last nod, whispered, 'Be good!' and went through the kitchen and out into the shop.

I could hear him speaking in Italian to Mr and Mrs Moretti as he went, heard them talking back.

'He's gone to catch the train,' said Aldo.

'Yes,' said Freddo. 'Come on, we'd better go and eat.'

'You going to eat with us, Bob?' Aldo asked as we went back through the outhouse, past the empty ice-cream vats. In the kitchen, the table had been covered with a bright-coloured cloth and laid out with big brown dishes. In the middle stood a bowl of the white stringy stuff that Mrs Moretti had been cooking in the pan.

'Pasta!' said Aldo, eyes gleaming.

'Can Bob stay, Mamma?' Freddo asked. He and Al were washing their hands under the tap by the back door.

'I just had dinner,' I said, but my mouth was watering as the boys moved to the table. Freddo waited, his hand on the back of a chair that would be for me if his mother said yes.

She spooned the pasta into the brown dishes and poured a thick red juice over each one. 'You sure you wouldn't like some, Robert?' she asked. 'There's enough to go round.'

'All right then,' I said, and Freddo pulled up the chair for me to join them at the table. 'Thank you, Mrs Moretti.' I didn't need asking twice.

I washed my hands like I'd seen the boys do, and sat down next to Freddo.

Mrs Moretti went on spooning the pasta into the bowls. 'Pietro,' she called. 'You come and eat. I'll look after the shop.'

Mr Moretti shouted back, 'I'm coming.'

'You behave now,' Mrs Moretti warned us, and went out through the kitchen door, leaving the three of us slurping away.

I'd never had pasta before.

'It's spaghetti,' Freddo said, showing me the way to eat it. I wasn't very good. I couldn't stop the long strings from falling off my spoon, even with the fork they'd given me to keep it from slipping back into the dish. I made a lot of mess on the table.

Aldo and Freddo thought it was funny. So did Mr Moretti, who had come to sit with us. 'Don't worry, Roberto,' he said. 'It's an art! We'll teach you in no time. We'll have you eating like a true Italian.'

Freddo looked at him. 'Papa!'

I'd never heard him call his father 'Papa' before. Not outside, where people could hear, anyway. Aldo did, but never Freddo.

'Oh, sorry, Roberto.' Mr Moretti raised his hand to his mouth, and his eyes went big and wide. 'Maybe not the right thing to say. Under the circumstances.' He chuckled to himself, then we all went a bit quiet.

Not for long, though. A few more splashes from me, and Aldo burst out laughing. 'You got a bloody shirt, Bob.'

I squinted down at my chest and saw that the red juice had splattered itself across my shirt front like a trail of blood.

'Bob's got a bloody shirt, Papa.' Aldo liked saying it.

He roared with laughter, Freddo joining in, Mr Moretti smiling, raising his finger to his lips to shush the two of them.

The kitchen door opened and Mrs Moretti came through from the shop, her face whiter even than before. She closed the door behind her, hard.

'Sorry, Mamma,' said Aldo, trying to fight down his laughter, but still eating.

She ignored him, looked straight at me. I thought maybe she wanted me to apologise for the mess, but it wasn't that. 'I think it's time you were going home, Robert,' she said.

'Oh, Mamma, he wasn't doing it deliberately . . .' Freddo came to my defence, but his mother stopped him.

'Robert should go home, Frederico.' She looked as if she was about to burst into tears. 'Now, please.'

I didn't understand what was happening, but I put down my fork and spoon, pushed back my chair and got up from the table.

So did Mr Moretti. 'What's this about, Lena? What's going on?' Then he started in Italian, while I stood there, not able to get past him and out of the kitchen.

Mrs Moretti began to cry, but only for a moment. She stopped, dabbed at her eyes, replied in Italian. Something urgent, upsetting.

The boys stopped eating. Freddo got to his feet, as white-faced now as his mother.

Then, from the shop came a man's voice. 'Mrs Moretti!'

The man called out again, 'I'll have to come in, if Mr Moretti won't come out.'

More whispered conversation between the grown-ups. Italian, so I couldn't understand.

Aldo stopped eating, looked from one to another, his eyes big with concern.

The man in the shop called out a third time, 'Did you hear me?'

'Yes, Gethin,' said Mr Moretti, voice raised. 'Won't be a minute.'

Gethin? PC Richards?

Mr Moretti made for the door, but his wife wouldn't let him reach for the handle. She stood, facing him, back planted firm against the wooden panels.

'Lena! Come on, love.' Mr Moretti pleaded with her, in English now: 'We'll have to speak to him.'

'I know that. But not yet!' And she burst into tears again.

Mr Moretti took her by the shoulders and settled her in one of the big chairs at the side of the stove. The boys looked on, scared.

'What is it, Freddo?' I asked, though I knew what his answer would be.

'The police have come for my papa,' he whispered.

'Didn't waste any time, did they?' Mrs Moretti dried her eyes and got up from the chair. She opened the door to the shop.

PC Richards was standing there with another policeman. They shifted on the spot, embarrassed. Mr and Mrs Moretti stood in the doorway, facing them. We three boys stood behind them like we were watching a film.

'Sorry about this, Pietro,' said PC Richards. 'But my orders are to take you down the police station.'

'Yes. I know,' Mr Moretti said, calm as anything.

'How long for?' asked Mrs Moretti.

'Don't know, Lena.' PC Richards was getting more and more embarrassed.

The other policeman coughed, the kind of cough that said, 'Come on, Gethin. Let's get this over and done with. Quick!'

'And where will you take him after that?' Mrs Moretti again.

'We haven't been told,' said PC Richards.

'A holding camp,' said the other man, who wasn't from round here, so didn't know the family and didn't care to treat them kindly like PC Richards was trying to do.

'An internment camp, you mean,' said Mrs Moretti. 'Let's be plain about it, yes?'

A big sob poured out of Aldo, standing by my side.

'Lena,' said Mr Moretti. 'You're upsetting the boys.'

'*I'M* upsetting them? *I'M* upsetting them!' Now she was angry and showing it. 'What about these two?' She pointed at the men in the shop. 'They're the ones who are doing the upsetting! Shame on you, Gethin Richards! We haven't done anything wrong. What have we done wrong? Eh?'

'That's enough of that now, missus,' said the other policeman. 'We're only obeying orders. Your husband is officially an enemy alien!'

Those words again.

'Enemy alien! Nonsense!' cried Mrs Moretti.

'Lena, this isn't helping,' said Mr Moretti and he placed his hand on his wife's arm.

She shrugged it away, but she didn't say any more.

'Frederico,' said Mr Moretti, reaching across for his jacket on a hook by the door. 'Go upstairs for me, will you?'

'Why, Papa?'

'In our bedroom . . . by the wardrobe . . . you'll find a small case. Bring it down for me, there's a good boy.'

Another huge sob from Aldo who had slumped back into his chair at the table.

'Do I have to?' Freddo asked.

'Yes,' said his father. 'There's a good boy.'

Freddo went up the staircase from the kitchen.

I stood still, not knowing where to look, not wanting to be there, really.

Aldo's face was wet with tears. His father tried to comfort him, coming over to where he sat, bending down, putting an arm round his shoulder. 'Shush, now. Shush,' he whispered in his son's ear. 'It won't be for long, my lovely Aldo. *Aldo bello.*' He kissed him on the forehead. 'I'll be back before you know it.'

'Will you, Papa? Honest?'

'I'll try. Now you have to be a good strong boy for your mamma.'

'Like Uncle Gino said,' sniffed Aldo.

'Did he?' Mr Moretti asked. 'Well, he's right.'

There were footsteps on the stairs and Freddo came down with a small brown suitcase. Mr Moretti must have been preparing for this.

He stood up and took the case and pulled Freddo to his chest. He held him there, hugging him tight. Freddo's body shook with crying.

'You be strong, Frederico,' Mr Moretti sniffed and tore himself away. 'For your mamma and brother.'

'Yes,' Freddo nodded, being brave. But then he wailed, 'Don't let them take you away. Don't go.'

Now both boys were sobbing out loud.

I looked out of the kitchen window onto the yard. I didn't want to see my friends like this.

I heard Aldo's loud whisper. 'We could help you escape, Papa. I could give you a bunk up over the back wall.'

'No, Aldo,' said Mr Moretti, laughing gently. 'I have to go. But it's only for a little while.' He spoke to the boys in Italian then, soft, soothing words.

Then he spoke to me. 'Roberto?' he said.

I turned away from the window and he came over, hand outstretched. 'Thank you for being such a good friend to my sons,' he said. 'I hope you'll be able to stay that way whatever happens.'

Tears sprang to my eyes now. 'Yes,' I mumbled. We shook hands and he moved to the door.

Mrs Moretti was standing there, still as a stone. She wasn't crying any more. Instead her face was hard with anger.

Mr Moretti spoke to her in Italian, gave her a big hug and kissed her on the forehead.

Then he walked into the shop. 'Come on then, Gethin. Lead the way!'

Chapter 19

When I got home I didn't tell Nanna what I'd seen. Didn't even tell her where I'd been. Couldn't face her questions, I suppose. I didn't want to tell her that when Mr Moretti got marched along the street to the police station, some people had pointed and laughed and some had cheered.

I didn't want to tell her how the boys clung on to their mam as they watched all this from the doorway of the shop.

I didn't want to tell her how relieved I was when Mrs Moretti said I really ought to be going home now, that they'd be fine, that the boys' papa would be back in no time at all.

I didn't tell my mam any of this either when she got home from the factory.

I definitely didn't tell Reg when he came breezing in from playing with his mates and his 'best butty' Ivor Ingrams.

They all knew what had happened, though. It was big news. All the Italian men from all the Italian cafés in the villages round here had been marched off to the police station.

'Then they took them away in one of Tommy Vowles's coaches,' my mam said.

'*Duw, duw*,' said my nanna, shaking her head.

134

'There's terrible for poor Lena. Where did they take them, Myra?'

My mother didn't know. Reg didn't either. For once.

Freddo and Aldo knew, though. They told me next morning on the way to school.

Though Aldo himself had already left school, he'd usually walk along with us, keeping us company, before going back home to help out in the shop.

'They've taken them to England,' Freddo said. 'A place called Bury.'

'Uncle Gino's gone there, too,' added Aldo, balancing on the kerb.

'But you told me he promised to be loyal to the King,' I said.

'Aye,' Freddo went on. 'But they've taken them all so they can look at their papers and things and then decide what to do with them.'

We'd reached the school gate. A small crowd of boys hung around. Ivor and Billy and Trevor Davies, and Vic, who was swinging on the high iron gate. They'd been watching us coming for a while, nudging each other, whispering.

'Didn't expect to see you this morning, butt,' said Ivor to Freddo as we came closer.

Trevor grinned. Billy looked at me to see how I'd react. Vic carried on swinging to and fro, his eyes fixed firmly on the ground.

We stood on the pavement facing them. 'Why not?' Freddo said. 'It's a school day.'

He gave Aldo a little push in the direction of their shop.

'Oh, aye,' said Ivor. 'But I thought you'd both be looking after your mam. Now your dad's gone on holiday with all his other Eyetie friends.'

The others laughed. Vic stopped swinging.

Freddo scowled, but he didn't say anything. He gave Aldo another little push along the pavement. 'See you later, Al. Go back to the shop now.'

'A'right, Fred.'

'Don't let any one get at you, mind,' Freddo added.

'I won't.'

'Right! See you then.'

'See you.'

It was Ivor who shouted as Aldo walked away. 'How old are you now, butt?'

'Shut up, you!' Freddo launched himself at Ivor, but Ivor just dodged past him and slipped into the school yard. He pushed Vic off the gate and slammed it shut between him and Freddo.

'Oi! Mind!' Vic shouted, picking himself up.

Aldo had stopped, turned around. 'You all right, Fred?' he called.

Freddo was gripping the bars of the gate, shaking them, furious, as Ivor held the gate shut. 'Yes. You go home, Al,' he shouted down the street.

But Aldo was already making his way back along the pavement, calling out, 'Do you want me to help you open the gate?'

Now other boys came running across the yard, excited, hoping for a fight. They stood and watched from inside the railings, lined up behind Ivor. Gwenda

136

Lewis came round the corner of the school wall and busied along to see what was happening.

'Go home, Al,' Freddo shouted again, but Aldo had joined us now, standing next to me, looking on.

'I can open the gate, Freddo,' he said. 'I'm stronger than Ivor.'

'That's because you're older than me,' Ivor jeered, holding tight to the iron bars. 'How old *are* you, butt?'

'He's fifteen,' Gwenda chirped.

'Trust you to know,' Billy said.

'My father told me. It's his job to know these things.' Gwenda turned to Freddo. 'Well he is, isn't he?'

'Yes,' muttered Freddo, giving the gate another shake, face to face with Ivor through the bars. 'What's it to you, anyway?'

'Just thinking how lucky he is, in 'e?' Ivor sneered back. 'If he was *sixteen*, he'd be off on holiday as well.'

There were some more laughs at that.

'What's he mean, Fred?' Aldo asked, looking at Ivor, just waiting for the word to go and shake him off his perch.

'Nothing, Al. I don't know. Go home, will you?' Freddo gave the gate one last shake and moved away. 'Go on.'

'Only if you're all right.'

'I'm all right. I'll get even with him later, don't you worry.'

'I'll help,' Aldo said and he turned away, along the pavement, going home.

Gwenda Lewis walked off too, now that the argument seemed to be coming to nothing. 'They could be rounding up some of the younger boys next,' she offered as her parting shot. 'That's what my father said, anyway.'

Further up the street, Aldo heard her, stopped, and turned to look at Freddo. His eyes were big, startled, scared.

Freddo shouted, 'Don't listen to her, Al. She dunno what she's talking about. Go on home.'

Aldo hesitated, gave his brother a sad little wave and walked on.

Freddo turned on Gwenda. 'You're such a know-all, you are,' he hissed. 'Clear off!'

'No need to be rude. I'm only saying . . .'

'. . . *what my father said*,' Billy and Trevor chorused.

And off she went, superior, head in the air. As she rounded the corner into Cardiff Road, she looked back, gave us a final haughty stare, and bumped into Reg who was coming the other way.

We laughed, but Gwenda seemed not to hear. Or pretended she didn't anyway. She was buttering up to Reg, apologising, giggling.

He was his usual smarmy self, pretending to be interested in what she was saying.

We couldn't hear, but from the way she looked at us and nodded in our direction, it was obvious that she was telling him all about what had happened. Then she pointed at Aldo, heading off down the hill towards the café, telling Reg, no doubt, what her father had said about rounding up the younger Italian boys next.

That's when Reg really became interested.

Mr Rees came out on the front step and rang the bell for morning school. 'Open that gate, Ivor Ingrams. What do you think you're doing?'

'Nothing, Mr Rees.' Ivor let go of the gate and ran like a greyhound into the school.

The rest of us followed, walking, Freddo and me side by side.

'Do you think it's true, Fred?' I asked. 'What Gwenda was saying?'

'No. She's only showing off, Bob,' said Freddo, calm as anything now. 'It'll be all right.'

I wished I could believe him. I wished I hadn't turned to look at the street as we went through the main door of the school.

And, most of all, I wished I hadn't seen the smirk on Reg's face as he watched Aldo walking off down the hill.

Chapter 20

In the afternoon of the next day there was more news of Mr Moretti.

'Our Uncle Gino told us,' Aldo said. He was standing on the pavement, helping Freddo and their mam put up a big cardboard sign in the shop window. It had new glass in it now. The men had been doing it when I'd called for Freddo on the way to school that morning.

BUSINESS AS USUAL the sign said, just like the little notice that Mr Moretti had put up, but this sign was much bigger with letters drawn in coloured ink. Freddo had done it. I could tell from the handwriting.

It was Aldo's job to say if the sign was straight or not. There were strings at each end to hang it from the top of the window frame.

'It's a bit down on this side,' he shouted.

Inside the shop, Freddo and his mam shifted the sign to straighten it up. 'How's that?' Freddo mouthed through the window.

Aldo squinted at the sign, tilted his head to one side. 'It's gone down too much the other way now,' he said.

More lining up from inside the window, more squinting from Aldo. 'What do you think, Bob?' he asked.

'I think it's all right, Al. Looks straight to me.'

'Bob thinks it looks straight,' Aldo shouted.

So Mrs Moretti reached up and tied the strings to a

couple of nails at the top of the window frame. Aldo looked on, approving.

'What about your dad, then, Al?' I asked. 'What have you heard?'

'He's in prison,' Aldo said. And he began to cry.

Mrs Moretti had finished tying the strings and looked at him through the window. She said something to Freddo, and quick as quick, Freddo was out on the pavement at his brother's side. 'What's the matter, Al?'

'He was telling me that you'd heard from your dad,' I said, a little bit embarrassed that I'd made Aldo cry.

'We've heard *about* him,' said Freddo, pulling a hankie out of his pocket and passing it to his brother. 'We haven't heard from Dad himself.'

'Uncle Gino told us, didn't he, Fred?' Aldo gave his nose a big blow in the handkerchief.

'Yes, Al,' Freddo said, giving his mother a nod through the window. It's all right, he was saying. Don't worry. She nodded back, checked that the sign was hanging straight, and moved out of the window into the shop.

Aldo gave another big blow in the handkerchief and passed it back to his brother. Freddo very carefully folded it up and put it in his pocket.

Then we all sat down on the step of the shop in the afternoon sun and Freddo told me what they'd heard. Mr Moretti wasn't in prison but, like all the other Italian men from round here, he'd been taken to an old cotton mill in Lancashire.

'That's in England,' Aldo said.

They were going to be sorted out there, and then

moved on to other places. The Isle of Man had been mentioned, and Canada.

'Is that far away, Fred?' asked Aldo. 'I don't want Papa to go far away.'

'Let's worry about that when we have to, Al.' Freddo reached across to stroke his brother's arm. 'Wait till we hear something more, eh?'

Truth was that nobody was very sure yet what was really going to happen next. Or so Uncle Gino had said when he'd spoken to his wife that morning on the telephone.

'My Auntie Edda came over to tell Mamma the news,' Aldo said.

After that the three of us didn't say anything for a bit, just sat on the step and watched people out and about. There weren't many around at this time of day. You had to do your shopping early now, because shops sometimes ran out of supplies later on.

'Hello, boys,' said Mrs Rees, as she passed. 'Not out playing then?'

'No,' we said. We didn't feel like playing, really.

At school, nothing had been said about what happened the day before, though Freddo had managed to trip Ivor up twice in the playground. 'Sorry, butt,' Freddo had said both times, pretending they were accidents. One of the teachers was looking on. Which meant that Ivor couldn't do anything, except scowl.

Reg hadn't made any of his clever remarks at home either, not even when Nanna asked me how Fred and Aldo were doing, now their father had been taken away.

142

'Shame, innit, Nan?' he'd said, looking straight at me when he spoke, his voice giving nothing away about how he really felt.

Mr Griffiths, the stationmaster, came puffing up the hill.

'Are you open, boys?'

'Yes, Mr Griffiths,' said Freddo.

'We made a sign, see?' Aldo pointed proudly at the cardboard hanging in the window.

'Very good,' said Mr Griffiths. 'Let me in then.'

We shuffled along the step and made a space for him to pass into the shop. We heard him asking Mrs Moretti if she had any tobacco.

'Seeing it's you,' she said, 'yes.'

'We're only selling it to regular customers,' said Freddo. 'Don't know how many of them we'll get now.'

'Let's go up the Pandy pool, Fred.' That was Aldo.

'Not now, Al.'

'Why not?'

'We'd better stay with Mamma for a bit.'

'Fair dos,' Aldo said, and the three of us shuffled apart again as Mr Griffiths came out the front door, tobacco in hand.

'You be good now, you boys,' he said as he walked back down the hill to the station.

'Yes, Mr Griffiths,' we chorused.

After that nothing much happened. Nobody else came by. A train whistle blew way down the valley. The pit winding-wheel turned and clanked in the distance.

Soon it would be time for afternoon school to finish and the evacuees would be piling into the street.

143

'There's PC Richards,' said Freddo.

He was coming along the street on the opposite pavement, with the other policeman who'd come to take Mr Moretti away.

Aldo gave a little cry and struggled to his feet, breathing heavily.

'It's all right, Al,' Freddo said, getting to his feet too, holding on to his big brother's arm, stroking it again, trying to calm his panic. 'Don't worry.'

I'd never seen Aldo like this before. Usually, nothing seemed to worry him, but now the sight of the two policemen was making him act really scared. Seemed like he'd believed everything Gwenda had said yesterday, about rounding up the younger boys.

'Are they coming here?' Aldo asked, trying to break away into the shop. He was getting more and more upset, but Freddo held on to his arm, tight.

'No, Al,' I said. 'They're keeping to the other side of the street. See.'

Aldo watched, stopped struggling with his brother.

The two policemen came closer and glanced in our direction. PC Richards looked a bit sheepish and gave an embarrassed nod. The other man just stared at us. Then they walked by without stopping.

'See, Al,' said Freddo. 'No need to get worked up.' He pulled his brother back down onto the step.

Aldo was calm again.

The Cardiff bus rolled by, someone waving from the back window. 'It's Billy,' said Freddo. 'With his auntie.'

'Bet she's taking him to the pictures,' I said. 'She's always taking him to the pictures.'

Aldo suddenly piped up, 'Let's ask Mamma if we can go to the pictures later. Shall we, Fred?'

'Maybe not, Al. Maybe we ought to stay in tonight.' He was obviously worried about his mother being on her own.

'Aw . . . let's ask, anyway.' Aldo struggled up from the step, his big body making him a bit unsteady. 'Not in Cardiff. Here. Up the Cosy. You come too, Bob. Will you?'

'If my mam lets me, Al,' I said.

He went into the shop, calling out, 'Mamma, can we go to the Cosy with Bob?'

Freddo laughed. 'He's making it look as if it's your idea.'

'I don't mind,' I said. '*Traitor Spy* is on. With Bruce Cabot. It's supposed to be good.'

'Perhaps it'll stop Al worrying,' Freddo said, turning serious.

'About your dad?'

He nodded.

'And what Gwenda said yesterday?' I went on. 'About them coming for the younger ones?'

'Yes. Specially that.'

'They won't,' I said. 'Will they?'

'I don't know. But it's put the wind up him. He thinks PC Richards will come for him next.'

'That's why he got himself in a bit of a paddy, then,' I said. 'Thought that was it.'

Mrs Pritchard came shuffling up the street in her slippers. She stopped to look at the sign in the window, sniffed and walked on.

Freddo got to his feet and called after her, 'The shop is open, Mrs Pritchard.'

'Won't be needing anything from you, thank you,' she called over her shoulder as she walked on. 'Not for a long time.'

Freddo muttered something under his breath. It sounded like *strega*. Then he looked at me and grinned. 'It's Italian for *witch*,' he said.

'That's her, all right. The old witch! Wish Aldo had squeezed the bottom out of her cat – and left it out!'

We burst into laughter, were still laughing when Aldo came back.

'We can go!' he yelled. 'Auntie Edda's coming over, so Mamma says we can go to the pictures.' He saw us laughing, and joined in, happier than I'd seen him all afternoon. 'What you laughing at?'

Chapter 21

I couldn't ask my mam if I could go to the pictures, because she was still at the factory, but Nanna said it would be all right. 'Be sure to be home before the blackout, mind.'

'Yes, Nanna.'

'And pour me a glass of pop before you go. Your mam said there was a little drop left.'

'Yes, Nanna.'

'I expect you'll be wanting some money, will you?'

'Yes, Nanna. Thanks.'

I took the bottle of lemonade from the food cupboard and poured the last of it in a glass. I put the glass in Nanna's hand.

'Lovely,' she said, taking a good long sip and smacking her lips. 'Nice and sharp.'

Then Reg breezed in from school and spoiled things. 'Hello, Nan. How's the spy network doing? Any messages?'

She chuckled, as usual, told him what a laugh he was, and then she said, 'Robert's going to the pictures, Reginald. Why don't you go with him? My treat.'

'No, Nanna!' I jumped in, quick. 'I'm going with Fred and Aldo.'

'Don't be so mean, Robert,' she said. 'One more won't make any difference. Do you want to go, Reginald?'

'Love to, Nan. Last time I went to the flicks back home, we couldn't hear half what was being said, 'cos there was German planes buzzing us.'

'*Duw, duw,*' said Nanna. 'There's terrible.' She put her glass of pop on the sideboard and took her battered old purse from her apron pocket. She fumbled around inside for the money.

'But, Nanna, Reg doesn't want to come with us!' I was almost shouting. 'He doesn't get on with Freddo and Al. He's glad Mr Moretti's been taken away.'

Reg stared back, brazen-faced, smirking. 'Wouldn't say I was glad, butt. But these things happen in wartime, don't they, Nan?'

'Oh aye, they do, more's the pity,' she said, barely listening, fingering the money she'd pulled out of her purse. 'There's a wise boy you are.' She held out her hand with two threepenny pieces in the palm. 'That should get you in. Off you go. And no more bickering, Robert.'

So, that's how we left it. Except that, as we went up the street to the Cosy Cinema, he ran on ahead of me, and said as he passed by, 'Don't worry, butt. Won't be sitting with you and your little Eyetie friends. There'll be plenty of my mates there, I expect.'

There were too. When the lights went up after the adverts, and people were moving around noisily to get better seats before the big picture started, Freddo nudged me and said, 'Ivor Ingrams is back there.'

I turned in my seat, looking for him in the crowd. The cinema was nearly full. Downstairs anyway. We couldn't see upstairs where the pricey seats were. The air was hot and sweaty in the warm summer evening, and thick with cigarette smoke.

Ivor and his friends were sitting about six rows behind us. They were leaning over the seats in front of them, teasing some girls by playing with their hair. The girls were pretending to be annoyed, but they giggled and pulled faces at each other.

'Yes,' I said. 'Ivor's there. With his evacuee. Norman.'

'Pee-in-the-bed,' Aldo murmured, sucking on one of the sweets his mam had given us when we'd left the shop.

'And Reg?' Freddo said.

'Of course,' I said. 'Nanna gave him the money.'

Reg saw us then and whispered to the others. They looked at us and laughed.

I turned around to face the front. The lights were going down again, and the curtains were beginning to part. The beam of light from the projector cut through the smoky air, flickering on its path to the screen.

'Sit down, will you!' a man shouted, as people moved into the row behind us. 'You're not made of cellophane. Can't see through you.'

'Take it easy, mister,' someone shouted back. Seats thumped down as they settled themselves. 'Don't you know there's a war on?'

A few people laughed at that. Others shushed. 'It's the news,' Aldo said, nodding at the screen. They always showed the news before the big picture.

First thing on it was the German army in France. Now that they'd taken over the northern part of France, they were heading for Paris, or so the newsman

149

said. We saw tank after tank, truck after truck, trundling along straight, tree-lined roads. PARIS, a signpost had written on it. Some German soldiers looked at the camera, pointed in the direction of the sign and laughed.

Then we saw a newsreel of people leaving Paris, all ages, with suitcases and their belongings tied up in bundles, heading out along the roads, away from the advancing German armies.

'Bleeding cowards,' Reg called out, suddenly close.

I turned round to see that he and his friends must have moved forward when they saw us come in. They were now sitting in the row behind us.

'Should 'a' stayed to fight.'

A couple of people laughed; others agreed with him.

There was the noise of seats tipping up as someone moved towards the gangway. People muttered and cursed.

'Sorry! Sorry!' said a voice as the figure moved along the row, treading on feet. 'Got to go to the lav.'

'It's Norman,' Freddo leaned across to whisper.

'He's going for another pee,' said Aldo.

'Should have gone before you sat down,' Freddo piped up, loud enough for them to hear in the row behind.

Someone kicked the back of our seats. We swivelled round, the three of us, but Reg and Ivor were sitting looking up at the screen, all innocent. Even though we kept on looking at them, their eyes didn't move, not for one moment. Then Reg said, still without looking at us, 'Oi, Freddy boy. It's your lot! Look!'

We turned back to the screen. The newsreel had moved on. Now there were pictures taken in London. Little groups of people were standing around in the street, staring at shop windows that had been smashed in.

Aldo choked on his sweet. 'It's like our shop, Fred,' he whispered, wide-eyed.

Mobs had been attacking Italian shops and offices, said the newsman, now that Mussolini had finally decided to come into the war on Hitler's side. Like the Morettis, the shop owners had been putting up signs. 'THIS ESTABLISHMENT IS ENTIRELY BRITISH' said one. 'CARRYING ON AS USUAL' said another.

'More's the pity,' said a voice, very close behind us. Reg was leaning forward, poking his sly face into the gap between me and Freddo.

'Wonder if they'll show us where your daddy is?' Reg taunted.

'Shut up, you,' Freddo hissed, not turning round.

'Aye, leave it alone, Reg,' I backed him up, a bit weakly. I didn't know what was going to happen here.

'Be quiet, you boys,' said someone close by. 'Or I'll have you thrown out.'

'You and whose army?' Reg shouted back, and then he leaned forward, spreading his arms across the top of our seats.

The newsreel had moved on again. Now, police were guarding little groups of men, Italians, and shepherding them to waiting buses.

Aldo sat up straight in his seat, eyes fixed on the screen.

'Oh look,' sniped Reg. 'It's your papa!'

'Where? Where?' Aldo craned forward, sort of whimpering, getting more and more upset. I'd never seen him as bad as this before. Not lovely, laughing Aldo, kind Aldo, Aldo who would always try to cheer you up.

'It's not your dad, Al,' I said. 'He's not there. Don't listen to him.'

'That's in London, Al.' Freddo tried to calm his brother.

'If you can't be quiet, go home,' a man shouted three rows back.

'Yes. You'll be safer at home,' Reg taunted Aldo. 'You'll be able to barricade yourself in when the police come to get YOU!'

Ivor sniggered, half leaned forward, but didn't want to get too close, just in case.

Freddo sprang up, turned round and knocked Reg's arms off the back of the seat.

Reg pulled back, quick, mocking. 'It's true though, butt, ain't it? You heard what that Gwenda said about rounding up the younger kids. His turn next, eh?'

Freddo was up on the seat now, one leg over the back.

Reg stood too. Ivor sort of crouched, half-standing, half-sitting. Aldo stood up. I thought he was going to help Freddo, like he always did, but no. He edged towards the end of our row, treading on people's feet in his hurry to get out.

'Ow!' people went, and 'Mind out, will you!' and 'Take it easy, chum', as Aldo shuffled towards the gangway. Then there was shouting from the rows behind. 'Behave, will you!'

'Sit down!'

'I'm going,' Aldo called back to us.

'A'right, Al,' Freddo said, but by now, he'd got into the row behind and had started tussling with Reg. 'See you later,' he grunted, as Aldo made for the exit.

I was on my feet too, ready to climb over the seats and deal with Ivor if I had to. I was hoping it wouldn't come to that, though. Ivor was bigger than me.

A shaft of light hit us full in the face. Mrs Vickers, the usherette, was storming down the gangway, torch held high, pinning us in its beam.

'What in heaven's name is going on here?' she shouted.

Freddo and Reg couldn't take much of a swipe at each other because they could barely move in the narrow space, but Reg, bigger, stronger, seemed to have Fred pinned against the back of the seat.

There was pandemonium now. People were shouting, some standing up to get a better view in the half dark. From behind us, a girl screamed as she tried to get up from her seat. 'He tied my hair to the chair,' she wailed, doubled up, pinned to the seat, pointing at Reg.

Someone laughed.

Mrs Vickers was a big woman. She plunged into the row, crushing more feet, still shining her torch on the scrapping boys. She pushed Ivor aside, got hold of Freddo's shirt and started dragging him away. He was snarling with rage.

Mrs Vickers reached the end of the row, and marched

Freddo up the gangway towards the doors. I followed on.

'I'll be back for the rest of you,' she called behind her. There were a few cheers and claps.

I saw Reg pretend to settle down again, cocky, but keeping a lookout for the return of Mrs Vickers. As he turned to the people behind him, I heard him say, 'Dunno why she's blaming me. It was all his fault. Can't trust these Continental types, can you? Too bleedin' temperamental.'

Then I felt a tug on my sleeve and Mrs Vickers dragged me through the door, out of the darkness and into the light of the entrance hall. 'OUT!' she said. 'The pair of you!'

Freddo was nearly through the front doors anyway, red-faced and angry.

'I'm surprised at you two,' said Mrs Vickers, putting her torch down on the shelf of the pay box. She patted her hair back into place where it had come loose a bit in the struggle. 'Especially you, Frederico, what with your father being taken away. Thought you'd stay out of trouble for your mam's sake at least.'

'He started it,' sniffed Fred, slamming through the front doors of the cinema. 'He always starts it.' And he stormed out down the steps and into the sunny evening street.

Chapter 22

'Who's that?'

Damn! I'd opened and closed our front door quiet as anything, not wanting Nanna to hear, but she had. 'It's me, Nanna,' I called from the passage. All I wanted was to go up to my bedroom, not talk to anyone about what had happened.

'You're back early, love.'

'Yes.'

'Why's that?'

'Film wasn't much cop, Nanna.' I had my foot on the bottom stair.

'Well, come in here and tell me about it then.'

'Nothing to tell, Nanna.' Foot on second step now.

'Robert! I gave you the money to go, didn't I? You can have some manners and come in here and tell me about it. Come on.'

'A'right,' I sighed. 'But there's nothing to tell.' I went into the kitchen. Nanna was sitting by her wireless, as usual, listening to a play. People with posh voices having an argument. She turned the sound down a bit and looked to where she expected me to be. I stood in the doorway, itching to escape.

'What was the picture about?' she asked.

'Spies,' I said.

'Why didn't you like it then? You like spy pictures, don't you?'

'Usually, yes.' I hoped she wasn't going to ask me to tell her the story, because, of course, we hadn't been in the cinema long enough to see the big picture.

She didn't though. Instead, she asked, 'Didn't the Moretti boys like it?'

'No, Nanna. We came home together.'

That was a lie. When Freddo went running down the steps of the cinema, he hadn't waited for me. He'd just kept on running. 'See you tomorrow, Bob,' he'd shouted, not even bothering to turn and look back. I let him go. I knew he was worried about Aldo.

Behind me, our front door opened and closed with a bang. 'Anyone at home?'

Reg!

'We're in the kitchen,' Nanna shouted, sitting up a bit in her chair and wiping her mouth with her hankie.

'Righty ho!' He came along the passage, cheerful as anything, and pushed past me into the room. I got an elbow in my ribs as he squeezed by. 'Hello, Nan.' He pulled up one of the kitchen chairs and sat beside her. 'Has Robert told you about all the palaver in the flicks?'

She half turned in her chair, eyes seeking out his face. She wouldn't have been able to see his smirk. 'No,' she said. 'What was that, Robert?'

'Nothing, Nanna.'

'Nothing!' Reg whooped. 'His Italian friends only got us thrown out, that's all.'

'Whatever for?' Nanna pretended to be shocked but I could tell she was already warming into another of his little stories.

'For fighting, Nan,' he said. 'That's what.'

'Oh, there's shameful. What with their father being taken away and everything.'

'It is, Nan. Couldn't agree more. You'd think they'd behave themselves for their poor ma's sake, eh?'

'Who were they fighting, then?' Nanna asked.

'Me, Nan. Jumped over the seats they did. Can't take a joke, that Freddy boy.'

'You weren't making jokes,' I said. 'You were saying things to make Aldo scared.'

'I was joking, Rob. Only joking. Honest.' He looked at me, smiling, but not in his eyes.

'So who threw you out?' Nanna chipped in, eager for more details.

'That big woman,' he said. 'The one with the torch. And I don't mean bleedin' Florence Nightingale!'

Nanna liked that, laughed out loud. 'You're talking about Bella Vickers,' she said. 'Oh, you don't want to mess with her.'

'I didn't, Nan. I could tell what she was made of.'

'You didn't see much of the big picture, then?'

'Didn't see any, Nan. Got chucked out before it started.'

'Robert saw it though,' she said, turning back to me, still standing in the doorway. 'Didn't you, Robert?'

'Only a bit,' I muttered, lying.

Reg was enjoying this, seeing how uncomfortable I was.

'How d'you manage that then, butt? You got thrown out before me.'

'Never you mind,' I said, feeble as anything. 'None of your business.'

'Must be able to see into the future, eh, Nan?' Reg teased. 'Sees things before the rest of us do.'

Nanna had lost interest now. She turned back to the play on the wireless, but not before Reg said, 'I'll pay you back, Nan. Don't want you to think you've been throwing your money away.'

'Oh, there's a good boy you are,' she said, reaching out, fumbling for his hand and patting it gently. 'Don't you worry about that,' she said. 'I'm only sorry you got thrown out through no fault of your own.'

'NANNA!' I yelled. 'He's lying!' I couldn't hold back any longer. 'He started it! It was him, being horrible to Aldo. Making him frightened.'

'Hey!' she came back at me. 'That's enough of your shouting. You can go to bed if that's how you're going to behave.'

'Right!' I said, turning out of the room. 'That's what I want to do.'

'Good!' said Nanna. Then, to Reg, more quietly. 'He's gone very nasty since his father went away.'

I'd reached the bottom of the stairs. 'It's nothing to do with Dad,' I shouted. 'It's him. He's the one who's making me nasty.'

I took the stairs two at a time. I didn't want to hear any more of Reg or see the way he cosied up to Nanna.

I'd nearly got to the landing when the front door opened downstairs and my mam came in.

'Is that you shouting, Robert? We could hear you halfway up the street.'

There was someone with her, someone standing by the front door. From the landing I couldn't see who it was.

'He's in a terrible mood, Myra,' Nanna shouted from the kitchen. 'He needs a good telling-off.'

'All right, Mam. I'll deal with him later.' She walked into the passage a few steps, the other person following on behind. Then I saw who it was. Freddo!

'Frederico's with me, Mam,' my mother said, explaining that we had a visitor. 'He wants to know if we've seen Aldo. He's gone missing.'

Chapter 23

'He didn't come home,' Freddo said, closing the front door behind him and walking further into the passage. 'From the pictures.'

My mam called up the stairs, 'Frederico thought he might be with you, Robert.'

'No. I haven't seen him.'

'*Duw, duw,*' I heard Nanna say. 'Where's he gone then?'

My mother walked into the kitchen, Freddo following. Me too, leaping down the stairs to hear more.

'Hello, Reg,' my mother said, flopping down in a chair by the table, facing Freddo now, standing in the doorway.

Reg moved across to sit beside her. 'Evening, Mrs Prosser. You look tired.'

'I am, love. *You* haven't seen Aldo, have you?'

Freddo chipped in, quick, 'Not since he scared him out of his wits.'

'It was only a joke, butt,' Reg said. 'Can't you lot recognize a joke when you hear one?'

'Didn't sound like a joke,' Freddo snapped back.

'That's enough of that,' said my mother, striking a match and lighting up a cigarette. 'Stop arguing, the pair of you.' She blew out the match and threw it into the empty grate. 'Where've you been looking?' she asked Freddo.

'All round the streets,' he said. 'And Mamma and Auntie Edda went up the pit to see if anyone had seen him up there.'

Nanna switched off the wireless and leaned forward. 'Have your mam been to see Gethin Richards?'

'No,' said Freddo. 'She doesn't want to go to the police. Not yet.'

He turned to look at me, standing by his shoulder. We both knew that PC Richards wasn't Mrs Moretti's favourite person.

Reg piped up, 'Bet I know where he is.'

'Where's that then, Reg?' my mother asked.

'Bet he's up that pool you go to.' He looked at us across the kitchen, a little smirk on his face.

'Pandy pool?' said Nanna. 'What would he be doing there this time of night?'

'Bet he's in that cave, hiding,' said Reg, centre of attention now, pleased as anything. 'My mate Ivor told me about it. Says it's a regular little den for you and your friends.'

My mother got up from the table, and stubbed out her cigarette in the grate. 'Do you think he might be up there, Frederico?'

'Might be,' Freddo said, a bit unsure, not wanting to admit Reg could be right. 'I'd better go and have a look.'

'I'll come with you, Freddo.' I half turned into the passage, ready to make a getaway before my mother could stop me.

Sure enough, she tried to. 'You haven't had your supper yet,' she said, reaching up to get the plates out of the cupboard by the bosh.

'It's that late, is it?' Nanna said. 'I could do with something to eat, My. Haven't had anything . . .'

I interrupted her. 'Aw, come on, Mam. Freddo shouldn't go by himself.'

'No, Robert. It's getting late and I don't want you two up there on your own.'

She counted out the plates and put them on the table. Reg laid them out and reached into the drawer for the knives and forks. Ever so helpful he was! 'I'll go with them if you like, Mrs Prosser,' he said. 'I'm older than them. I'll get them home safe and sound.'

'Well . . .' Mam took the knives and forks from him. 'That would be . . .'

'NO!' Freddo shouted, seeing what was coming. 'Don't need his help, thanks.'

'Mam,' I pleaded. '*He's* the one who started all this. That's why Aldo's gone missing.'

'Well, this'll be a chance for him to make things up then,' my mother said, and, turning to him, she added, 'won't it, Reginald?'

'Course, Mrs P,' he smarmed.

This was turning out just like the night when I'd had to take Reg with me to look at the crowds attacking Moretti's café. But I could see that it was going to be the only way I'd be allowed to go and look for Aldo.

I tried one last time. 'It'll be curfew time for the evacuees in a minute. Reg shouldn't be out.' Even as I said it, I knew he'd come back with a smart answer.

'You're right there, Bob. But this is a bit of an emergency, ain't it?'

He straightened out the last of the forks my mother

had laid out on the table. 'No one would want to stop me doing my little bit for the war effort.'

'Like with the parachutist?' Freddo muttered, but loud enough for Reg to hear. His face flared red but he stayed silent.

'I don't know what you're all on about,' said my mother, putting pans on the gas stove ready to start the supper. 'But if you're going, you'd better go soon. Otherwise it'll be dark, and you're definitely not going then.'

Freddo and I looked at each other. 'A'right, Fred?' I asked.

He nodded back. 'Yeah. A'right. Let's go.'

Chapter 24

Through the streets we ran, fast as anything, me and
Freddo trying to outpace Reg. We dodged in and out of
all the back alleys, trying to lose him, throw him off our
tail.

We didn't, though. He always caught up with us.

Freddo had stopped at the café to tell his mam and
his auntie where we were going. Me and Reg waited
outside, not saying anything, not even looking at each
other.

There were plenty of people about, enjoying the
remains of the sunny evening.

'Hello, Robert.' Mr Yoxall was out with Mrs Yoxall.

'Hello, Mr Yoxall,' I said. 'No news of my dad.'

I knew that's what he'd have asked, and before he
could carry on with 'no news is good news', Freddo
charged out of the café door, yelling back, 'Won't be
long, Mamma. We'll find him.'

Then we were off again, running fit to bust until we
left the streets behind and we were haring across the
hilly fields that led up to the Pandy. Under the trees we
went, over the stile, and along the path, in and out of
the long, long shadows spilling across the ferns.

Reg was a good runner, I'll give him that, so by the
time we got to the top of the rocky ledges that
overlooked the pool, he was right there with us.

'AL!' Freddo yelled, puffed now, trying to get his breath back.

'*AL . . . AL . . . AL!*' came the echo from the quarry walls.

Freddo started to clamber down to the water's edge over the flat, smooth rocks.

'AL!' he called again. 'Are you there?'

'*There . . . there . . . there?*'

The two of us were scrambling down behind him, heading for the cave. Then he stopped, turned and spoke to Reg, 'YOU wait here. And don't move! If he sees you, that'll upset him worse.'

Reg stopped, steadied himself on the rocks. 'OK, butt, OK. Keep your hair on.' He sat down as Freddo gave him one last stare before the two of us moved forward.

We were by the water now, edging towards the cave, Freddo quietly calling, 'Al! It's Freddo. And Bob. Are you there?'

We stopped, listened. Not a sound.

The sun had started to slip away over the rim of the quarry. The light was grey and purple down by the pool, except where the still water reflected the sunset. Green and orange it looked, shading away into blackness. The top of the crane towered over it, ghostly, like some kind of creature.

We'd never been up the Pandy this late before. It felt a bit scary.

'Al?' Freddo tiptoed nearly to the mouth of our cave. 'Al? Are you in there?'

'Yes,' came a little voice.

Freddo stopped still.

'Can we come in, Al? Me and Bob?'

'Yes.'

'Here we come then.' Freddo moved on, waved for me to follow.

We peered into the mouth of the cave. We could hardly see Aldo at first. He was sitting in the gloom towards the back. He didn't seem to have anything with him, so if he was going to stay in there, hiding, he didn't seem to be prepared for it.

Freddo went down on his hands and knees and crept towards his brother. I held back, waiting to see what would happen.

'What you doing here, Al?' Freddo asked. He reached out and stroked Aldo's arm.

'Hiding.'

'What for, Al?'

'Case they come for me. Like with Papa.'

'No one's going to come for you. Are they, Bob?' Freddo gave me a little wave to bring me to where they were both sitting.

'Course not, Al,' I said, clambering forward. 'Don't believe anything Reg says. He's a troublemaker.'

'But Gwenda Lewis said her father said . . .'

'She's just a know-all, Al,' said Freddo, still stroking his brother's arm. 'She *thinks* she knows everything, but she doesn't.'

'They're not going to come for the boys, then?' Aldo brightened up a little now.

'No,' said Freddo. 'They're not.'

166

'Promise, Fred?'

'Promise, Al.'

Then Freddo whispered something in Italian, words that made soft, soothing sounds. Sounds like Mr Moretti whispered to the boys when he was being taken away. Sounds that made Aldo smile.

'You coming home now, Al?' Freddo asked. 'You going to be strong for Mamma?'

Aldo nodded. 'Like Uncle Gino said.'

'Yes.'

'A'right then.' Aldo flexed his arms, pretending to show off his muscles.

Then he laughed and beat his chest. 'ME TARZAN! Me big and strong!'

Great! The old Aldo was back, lovely, laughing Aldo. We were laughing too, relieved and happy.

There was a sound from outside the cave. Small stones, dislodged, falling in the water. Aldo stopped laughing, was wide-eyed, alert.

Freddo said, quick as a flash, 'It's all right, Al. Nothing to worry about.'

But Aldo could see what we saw. The figure of Reg, peering round the entrance to the cave. Aldo whimpered, a sad, frightening sound, like he'd made in the pictures.

Freddo tried to calm him. 'We had to bring him with us, Al. Bob's mam said. But he won't hurt you.' Then he turned, quick as anything, and scrambled towards the mouth of the cave. 'I TOLD YOU TO KEEP OUT OF THIS!' He'd reached the entrance, Reg still looking in. 'YOU NEVER DAMN WELL LISTEN, DO YOU?'

And he gave Reg an almighty push that sent him reeling backwards, big as he was. It was Freddo's anger that gave him the strength to do it, I think.

We heard Reg shout as he disappeared from view. We heard the scrabbling of feet. A splash, another shout. Then we heard Freddo laugh.

There was more shouting.

Aldo and me crawled, fast as anything, up to the mouth of the cave.

'He's in the water,' Aldo grunted as we straightened up at the edge of the pool. 'Reg fell in the water.'

'He slipped,' said Freddo, still laughing, pointing at Reg, floundering and splashing and shouting.

We shouted too, laughing and yelping, enjoying the sight of Reg thrashing about.

He seemed to be drifting out towards the crane. 'Help me, will ya?' he gasped, taking in more water. 'I can't swim.'

'Aw, don't give us that,' I shouted back. 'You said you were a champion swimmer. Told us how great you were.'

The three of us jeered and laughed and Freddo yelled, 'You come from the seaside. Everyone can swim.'

'Not me,' choked Reg. 'Never learned. I was lying.'

That made us laugh even more, Freddo most of all. 'So . . . the big *I AM* can't swim,' he whooped. 'He's all talk!'

'All talk,' Aldo echoed, enjoying the joke. 'He really can't swim, can he, Fred?'

That was becoming obvious. Reg was thrashing

about more and more, drifting further from the edge of the pool.

Our laughter died a little bit. 'You're kidding, you are,' I shouted.

'Another one of your stories,' Freddo joined in. 'You just want to get one of us in there with you! Get your own back.'

'No! . . . I swear!' More gulps from Reg, more thrashing. 'I can't. Help me. PLEASE!'

Then his head went down. He slid away through the green-gold surface of the water, down into the blackness.

None of us was laughing now. 'He's having us on,' Freddo said, a bit nervous. 'Just you wait.'

Almost as soon as he finished speaking, Reg bobbed up again, spluttering and coughing and crying. At the very end of his breath, he pleaded with us, 'Please! . . . Help me!'

He slipped away again into the blackness.

We three stood like statues, quiet, not believing what we were seeing. *The boy we hated was drowning in front of our eyes.*

And still we didn't move. We just watched. Frightened. Excited.

Aldo broke the silence. 'He's drowning,' he whispered.

'Yes,' Freddo said, almost as quiet.

'What are we going to do?' I asked, quiet too.

The silence grew in the shadows. Then, suddenly, Aldo shouted, 'I'll get him! I'm the best swimmer.'

And before Freddo and I could stop him, he leapt,

clothes on, into the water. His big, powerful arms broke the still surface of the pool until he reached the spot where we last saw Reg.

Down he dived, a trail of bubbles telling us where he was.

We waited, watching, saying nothing. Except that I sort of knew what Freddo was feeling. I felt it too.

We didn't know if we wanted Aldo to save Reg or to let him go.

Chapter 25

WHOOSH!

With a mighty yell, Aldo came surging up to the surface, gasping for breath, but with one arm round a coughing, spluttering Reg.

'I got him!' Aldo shouted. He was coughing too, but there was a light of triumph in his eyes. He kicked towards the pool edge, towing the whimpering Reg with him.

Freddo and I reached out as Aldo brought him close by, and together we pulled the shaking body onto the rocks.

Reg lay on his stomach, coughing up water, groaning. His long trousers clung to his legs. His shirt was torn. He'd lost a shoe.

Freddo leaned over and taunted him. 'Hope this'll teach you to be a bit more grateful now.'

Reg groaned. He spat out more water, coughing and choking at the same time. 'You p-p-pushed me!' he shivered.

Freddo spat back, bending close to Reg's ear. 'You *tripped!* I pushed you out of the cave – but I didn't push you in the water. Don't you ever say I pushed you in the water. Right, butt? Got that straight?'

Reg mumbled something. It might have been a 'yes'.

'Look at me! Look!' From behind us, Aldo bobbed up and down in the water.

'*Look! Look! Look!*' went the echo.

'Look, Fred,' Aldo said, laughing. 'Who am I being?' He bobbed about some more, but he was shouting now and waving his arms around. 'Help!' he cried, in a little voice. 'I can't swim. Help.'

He slipped down under the water, leaving one hand waving above the surface.

We shouted encouragement from the pool's edge. 'Very good, Al,' we yelled. 'Very funny!'

Aldo popped up again, further from the edge, being more dramatic this time. He thrashed his way back towards us. 'I'm Reg,' he spluttered. 'I'm drowning, I am.'

'You're daft, you are,' Freddo shouted, laughing.

'Funny, though,' I agreed.

Reg went on moaning where he lay.

'Well?' Freddo stood and looked down at him. 'In't you going to say thank you?'

Reg rolled over on his stomach. Water dribbled from his mouth. He grunted something we couldn't hear.

'You'll have to speak louder than that,' Freddo said.

Aldo had paddled up to the side of the pool now. He rested his arms on the stone blocks and looked at his brother. He was proud, you could tell.

'Thank you!' Reg lifted his head a bit and coughed out the words.

'Don't say it to me,' Freddo said, nudging Reg with his foot, making him turn over. 'It's my big brother you need to thank!'

Reg sat up, his wet red hair plastered tight to his head. He looked at Aldo, bobbing gently in the water, calm as anything now.

'Ta, mate,' he sniffed.

'Ta!' Freddo sneered. 'Ta? Is that all you can say? That's not a proper thank you, is it, Bob?'

'No,' I said, getting to my feet too, standing by his side.

Reg looked at us, but not with his usual smirk. He'd had a real scare and wasn't in the mood for being clever.

'Say "thank you, Aldo",' Freddo prompted. 'Go on! "Thank you, Aldo." Say it!'

Reg bowed his head, rubbed his arm to brush away some of the water. 'Thank you, Aldo,' he muttered.

'Look at him when you say it.' Freddo wasn't going to let this go, not now he was in control. 'Look at him. Or we might have to tell everyone how you nearly drowned 'cos you can't swim. *And how you had to be rescued by my brother.* That'll make you look good, won' it?'

Reg looked up sharpish now, first at Freddo and me, and then at Aldo.

'Thank you, Aldo,' he said, clear as a bell.

'That's all right,' Aldo said, pulling himself out of the water. 'Don't mention it.' He stood there, dripping from head to toe, smiling. Kind, gentle Aldo, eager to please. He padded over to his brother, clothes dripping, leaving a trail of water on the dark rocks. 'We couldn't have let him drown, could we, Fred? Even if we wanted.'

'No, Al. We couldn't.'

Freddo looked at me. I knew what he was thinking. Then he turned back to Reg. 'But things had better be a bit different from now on. Agreed?'

Another mutter. 'Yes.'

173

Freddo nodded, satisfied for now. 'Don' need to be afraid of him any more, Al. Right?'

'Right you are.'

It was nearly dark. 'We'd better go home,' I said. 'Before they send someone to look for us.'

'What'll I tell Mamma?' Aldo asked, as the three of us turned away from the water. 'She'll be angry because I'm all wet. She'll know I've been in the Pandy.'

'We'll tell her it was an accident, Al,' said Freddo, heading up the path. 'We'll say you tripped and fell 'cos it was getting late.' He stopped and touched his brother on the arm. 'Anyway, she'll be too happy to see you to get angry.'

He moved on, Aldo trailing behind.

I turned back and said, 'You coming? *Reginald*?'

Aldo laughed at that.

'You'd better, *Reginald*,' I added. 'Or Nanna will be worried!'

Freddo laughed too. The pair of them stopped and turned to see what Reg would say.

He got to his feet, slowly. Even in the shadows, we could see he was trembling, not just shivering from the cold water, but really trembling because he'd had such a big fright. 'You won't say anything, will ya?' he pleaded. 'You won't say what happened. You'll say it was an accident. Like with him!' He nodded at Aldo. 'You won' tell my mates. Will ya?'

Freddo and me looked at each other, deciding. Then Freddo turned to face Reg. 'Guess!'

Afterwards

We're waiting for Reg's mam to come today.

She'll be here on the five-past-two train. She's taking him home for a few days and then she's going to pack him off to Canada on a ship. She's heard about a scheme to send evacuees overseas.

She wrote to my mam to say that she thought he'd be happier there, because Reg didn't seem to be liking it quite so much in Wales these days. Pity, because he'd got off to such a good start.

As far as we know, Reg hasn't told anyone the full story of what happened up the Pandy.

We haven't either.

It's our secret. I suppose the three of us are still a bit worried that if the truth comes out, then Freddo will be blamed for pushing Reg too hard and nearly drowning him.

We all know that Reg could make it sound that way if he wanted to. He never has, though. Can't admit to needing help. Especially not from Aldo.

Oh, he still goes round his usual smirky self, palling up to Ivor and the rest, charming Nanna and my mam. But he never gets at me anymore, and he stays well clear of Freddo.

Doesn't laugh at Aldo either, not even when he told Reg that Mr Moretti was being sent to Canada too, until the war was over. Maybe they'd meet up there, Aldo had said.

*

There's a knock downstairs on the front door. I'm up in the bedroom.

Nanna calls out, 'Who's there?'

Reg rushes through the passage, saying, 'I'll get it, Nan. It's me ma, I hope.'

The door opens. There's lots of 'helloing' and 'how are you, son?' and 'good to see you, Ma', then he bounds up the stairs to get his case from my bedroom.

It's standing next to the fireplace, all packed. Reg picks it up, stares at me, looks as if he's thinking of something clever to say, then he's off down the stairs.

His mother must be in the kitchen, talking to Nanna, because he calls out, 'Ready, Ma.'

And as she says goodbye to Nanna and walks out of the front door with him, I can hear him raise his voice and say, 'Thank God you came, Ma. Glad to be shot of this place, I can tell you. Right little bunch of bullies they are!'

The door slams shut, but out in the street I can still hear him, talking loud so that I don't miss what he's saying.

'Just you wait till I tell you what happened at the Pandy pool.'